THE BEST CELLAR

THE
BEST
CELLAR

Charles Goodrum

ST. MARTIN'S PRESS
New York

Design by Claire Counihan

Library of Congress Cataloging-in-Publication Data

Goodrum, Charles A.
  The best cellar.

  I. Title. II. Title: Best cellar.
PS3557.059B4   1987   813'.54   87-1694
ISBN 0-312-00008-1

First Edition

10 9 8 7 6 5 4 3 2 1

THE BEST CELLAR

Chapter 1

O<small>N</small> Monday afternoon, the guide came out of her neat little brick building and bent over the Next Tour clock. She advanced the hand to three, straightened up, adjusted her uniform, and said, "Those of you who would like to join me in the mansion may assemble here on the walk, and we'll go up together."

The scattered couples all beamed their eagerness at the idea and started to drift toward the guide. Six, she counted. Three couples. She guessed two retired members of the Antique and Garden Club, an editor and his wife on their way to a convention in Washington, and a pair of blue-jeaned graduate students. The students were holding hands, with difficulty, in the boy's pocket. Sweet, she thought. I wonder if they're living together, and if so, how long will it last? The "editor" was looking at the guide and thinking what a shame it was to put such a splendid figure into such a flat uniform, and his wife was looking at the same uniform and thinking, God, that must be hot in the summer.

"As you can see, the house is one of the most beautiful

1

Georgian buildings in the country," the guide was saying. "It was built in 1741 and it still looks almost exactly the way it did when it first went up. Like all the great homes of Tidewater Virginia, it was oriented to the river. The owner came up the water looking for some land. He selected this promontory, and he brought in his workmen by boat. They cleared this spot out of the forest and built this terribly sophisticated building, which could have sat quite comfortably in Hyde Park, England." She was now turned a quarter toward their center of interest, but she was still standing firmly on the oystershell walk. Nobody was going anywhere until she was ready for them to move.

"The rivers were to the Tidewater plantations what the interstates are to us. Everything that was really going anywhere went by water. Every one of the three hundred great Virginia plantations had its own dock, and ocean-going ships would come right up to their own landing. The planter would walk out of his front door, go down his own walk and on to the ship—and when he stepped off again, he was in Bristol or London. It had a powerful impact on his thinking."

She smoothed the skirt across her hips, conscious of the editor's attention, and then started slowly toward the building.

"Practically everything you see came out of the land around us. The bricks were made of the clay dug out of the basement, and they were fired right over there." She pointed to a smooth stretch of well-mowed lawn. "The oak floors and the hemlock joists and beams came from the woods here. Even though it all looks terribly European, only the window glass and the locks and hinges were brought in. The doors and windows—everything— was made right here on the spot. Everything fit into its own hole. Nothing's the same size as anything else even though it all looks perfectly symmetrical."

She told her story very well, and while it was clear that

2

it was far from the first time she'd given it, she said it like it mattered. As she drifted toward the building, she timed her points to an exact match with the length of the curved driveway. At a discreet distance from the entrance she stopped and said, "Now I'd appreciate it if you would stay fairly close to me when we go inside. The house is still lived in by relatives of the original owners, and they have only made the downstairs available for our viewing."

This was too much for the students. "Wait a minute," the man said. "What do you mean, 'still lived in'? I thought this belonged to the state."

"Actually it does. The family gave it to Virginia about three years ago, but the two elderly ladies can live in it as long as they want to."

"Are they alone in there?" the retired wife asked.

"No, there's also a nephew living with them—but no servants, if that's what you mean." The guide's formality slipped slightly into a giggle, and she said, "Actually, the nephew disappeared over the weekend, and there is a slight flap going on. If someone comes out and looks at you very closely, don't be too surprised." She smiled to signal that it was of no great moment.

"Is the state giving the ladies something to live on?" the editor's wife asked.

Another broad smile. "No, that's hardly necessary. These are Brents, and though the family had a little diffi-culty after the Civil War—the plantation was down to about two thousand acres by 1880—they at least had their land, and they've been selling it off through the years and investing the money in more modern things. A Brent was the president of Southern Seaboard at one time, and they're all big in textiles. There's been a Brent on the board of Virginia Electric for generations. They are . . . very wealthy."

"Then why did they give up the house?"

The guide hesitated, apparently rejected a more politic

3

answer, and said, "When their brother died, the inheritance taxes would have been such a scr—such a shock, they unloaded the Hall to save themselves an enormous amount of money. Are there any questions about the mansion itself?"

"Yes," the editor said. "The house looks like Williamsburg. What is there about Williamsburg that always looks the same? We come from New England and our Salem and Deerfield houses were built at the same time these were, but they don't look like this. What makes a Williamsburg house look like Williamsburg?"

"Two things," the guide said. "Part real and part social. The reality is that Tidewater houses are built in a part of the country that is brutally hot most of the time. The houses had to have high ceilings and big windows and cross-ventilation to keep the heat from wiping out the owners. Mount Vernon still gets to over 100 degrees on the second floor most of the summer. The ground comes in here, too. Virginia houses are all built on clay, and they dug out the cellars to get material for the bricks. This also gave them a cool place to store food and wine, and by the time you put in a few windows so you can see in the cellar, you've jacked up 'Williamsburg houses' so they look sort of tall and patrician.

"New England houses were built for cold climates. Low ceilings, small windows. It's cold more of the time than it's hot. They sit on rocky soil and very few of them could have basements, so they sit low and rather firm on the ground. But there's a social element here, too. The Williamsburgers were very sympathetic to the English and they wanted to look as much like prosperous, well-heeled British as they could, so they copied the landed gentry's houses. Most of the New Englanders wanted no part of England—they'd fled from religious persecution or the Civil War or something, and wanted to look as different as possible. They went in for local materials built in utilitarian designs."

The guide looked toward the visitors' parking lot and frowned slightly at the sight of two tourists getting out of an expensive sports van. The pair started toward the house, making a wide arc along the trees, and the guide decided to add a few paragraphs to give the tourists a chance to join the group.

"The colonial Virginian tried to make everything neat and orderly. His houses are always balanced, his drives come right down the middle of the lot, the gardens are always symmetrical. He tried to keep all the social classes neat, too."

The editor smiled and asked, "And would you say it worked?"

The guide laughed. "No better than our way. The colonial Williamsburg papers are loaded with local crime, the economy was just as confused as ours . . . but I don't know . . . at least the clothes and the food and the furnishings were more graceful."

"But no murders, rapes, and muggings."

"Oh, yes. All three. I was reading George Wythe's biography just last week," the guide said. "You know, the Wythe of the Wythe house in Williamsburg—Jefferson and Marshall's law teacher. Did you know he died in agony? A teenage nephew found he was in Wythe's will and tried to hasten the bequest. He got a slave to help him poison the old man by pouring lye down his throat. Wythe lived a couple of weeks in incredible pain, long enough to disinherit the nephew. That was all, though. You couldn't be made to testify against yourself even in those days, and a slave's testimony didn't count, so the nephew got off scot-free!"

She looked toward the latest tourists to see how they were progressing and was surprised to find they had disappeared completely. Pivoting around, she could find no sign of them in any direction.

"Hmmph," she said. "All right. Let's go in."

She started up the half-dozen steps to the portico. "Why don't you join me in going back into the eighteenth century? Let your mind slip. Everything really is almost the same. This sharp smell of boxwood would have filled the air two hundred years ago just like it does now. The sound of our steps on the oystershells would have been the same. If we had been only men, we would have come on horseback and there would have been the smell of leather and sweaty horses. If we women had been along, we would have come in a cart or a coach and these would be creaking on their straps behind us, but still the smell of horses and box. There would have been seamen's shouts coming up from the river, and the rumble of tobacco barrels being rolled across planks into a ship down below . . ."

She inserted a huge brass key into the polished lock and turned the handle.

Chapter 2

Oɴ Tuesday, Betty Crighton Jones sat at her desk in the vaulted depths of the Werner-Bok Library and thought, "God, what a sublime way to get through life. And to think they're paying me for this."

She looked across at her work table, where six cans of the first motion pictures ever made were sitting, and she shook her head. "There's Fred Ott's *Sneeze* and I can run the frames through my fingers." Monday, Efram Perzach had kissed her hand, and she had gushed her thanks for his graceful introduction to the library's facsimile of the Brahms Violin Concerto. He had replied, "Ah, yes, Miss Jones. A lovely piece of music. I played it in Hamburg just last week. Hamburg is the very best place to play Brahms. Cold and foggy and damp. I was honored to help with your project." There were three Dürer etchings signed by the artist lying loose by the film cans. Jesus. What a way to make a living.

Yesterday, it was true, hadn't been so hot. She'd been hammered by incessant phone calls from people working the institution over for its acquisition of the Ransome family papers. Six big names from the Green Book had threatened to take *their* family records back, but by dint of low-keyed and patient diplomacy, everyone seemed to have calmed down, for the moment at least. While it was true that the Ransome family lived in a plywood teepee outside Taos and had deliberately torched a nursery school for publicity, all the kids had gotten out in time, and if you're trying to capture the story of American culture, surely the Ransomes represented the sixties as well as anyone. Think what the scholars could have done with the James family papers, if someone had saved them in time. Jesse, of course, not William and Henry. The Werner-Bok already had theirs.

No, the mix was marvelous. The curse, Crighton thought, was guilt and the pressure from her peers. She was twenty-nine. She'd brought off her first job with class but she'd been in it for three years now. Everyone said it was time to quit and move on. Why? If you don't, everyone will think you can't. You owe it to your career. Nobody works *for* you; you need supervisory experience. And when you're forty what will you wish you'd done today? Do you really want to spend your whole life being a public relations officer working in a Washington basement?

She sighed and looked up to see a stylish young woman step through her open door. Designer stuff if I've ever seen it, Crighton thought. Class. No garret scholar this.

"Miss Jones?" the woman asked. "I'm Durance Steele, and the folks at the Library of Congress suggested I come down to see you."

Crighton smiled and jumped up to pull the only other chair in the room away from the work table and set it beside her desk. She waved toward it. "Please sit down. What can I do for you?"

The woman eased into place, striking the long-legged

pose of a hosiery ad so gracefully that Crighton wondered if she were a model.

"My problem is," the woman said, "I need shelter." She flipped her hair back with a practiced snap. "I've come up to do a few weeks' research at the Library of Congress, and I need someplace I can stay without bankrupting myself in hotel rooms. I'd heard in Charlottesville that LC had rooms for scholars scattered around Capitol Hill, but now that I'm here they tell me everything's taken." Steele opened a sleek leather purse and extracted a slip of paper. "A Miss Claasson said that you might know of something here at the Werner-Bok."

"Lynda Claasson. Yes. Good kid. We trade thinking bodies back and forth." Crighton frowned and let her eyes go out of focus. "I think everyone on our list is full, too, but there's a grandmotherly type behind the Folger who's going to open up the middle of next week. We've placed a medievalist there and he's about to pull out." She laughed. "He's a funny little man. He's been creeping through one of our books of hours for a month now and either he's finally gotten to the end of it or his eyes have given out. Would you believe, he's been doing it a word at a time with a magnifying glass as big as a pie plate? Just lovely. What's your project?"

"I think I may have found a real time bomb in one of our national myths. Something quite startling, really."

"What period?"

"Jefferson Federal."

"Oh? What are you going to do with it? Is it a book? A paper?"

"No, I hope to roll it up and shove it into the conventional wisdom."

"Ummm." Crighton had never been overly sympathetic with the icon breakers, and she felt little interest in tripping a smarter-than-everybody lecture at this time of day.

On the other hand, the woman *was* rather unusual. She seemed totally miscast as a Jefferson scholar. She was beautifully made up, expensively dressed, and carried herself with the assurance of a Seven Sisters class president. "Where did you do your work?"

"U. Va."

"Really? I'd have guessed Vassar."

No response at all. No change of expression. Freeze frame silence.

Crighton found herself pricked with curiosity. What the hell, she thought, let's take a chance. Broaden the horizons.

"How does this grab you?" she asked. "What do you say you go up and check out the little old lady on the Hill, and if it looks right, go ahead and sign up for it, then stay with me until the room opens up. I've got an extra bedroom and you can get started on your research while you wait. I live out Massachusetts near American U. You can get in and out by bus quite easily. Do you have a car with you?"

"Yes, I drove up. It's in a lot near the Library of Congress."

"Good. Let me give you the address and you can check out the room, then come back here and we'll go to dinner. Either way you can tell me what you've decided while we eat. Does that make sense?"

"That would be most gracious of you, Miss Jones. I'll accept without a moment's hesitation. I'm assuming it wouldn't be too wildly inconvenient or you wouldn't have suggested it. Thank you. It's lovely of you."

"No strain. Let me get the details and you can get on with it."

Crighton copied off the essential data, handed it over, and Durance Steele disappeared, promising to be back in the basement office by five.

With the room cleared, Crighton checked the clock.

Three-thirty. She looked again at the day's correspondence and was reassured that she had either answered everything or gotten the queries into the right hands for an appropriate response. Only a single letter remained to be resolved. She took it in hand and started down the corridor for the elevator.

The Werner-Bok Library sits on the Mall exactly centered between the Smithsonian's Natural History Museum and the National Gallery of Art. Crighton took the elevator to the third floor where the various area studies reading rooms were distributed around the Great Hall. Stepping out of the elevator she turned left toward the National Gallery and the Capitol end of the building and headed for Asian Studies. Once inside she let her eyes become accustomed to the soft green from thick, hand-blown glass windows and headed for the division chief's office. Asian Studies had been designed with the rest of the building at the turn of the century, and to sustain the Far Eastern atmosphere, the architect had chosen Chinese Chippendale furniture, with lighted alcoves for porcelains and jades set at regular intervals along the walls. The effect had been good in 1898, and it had aged gracefully into our own time.

"Dr. Wu," she said, once seated opposite the chief, "we got a fairly nasty letter today from the Anglo-American Society of Oriental Studies. Here it is. As you'll see, they are insisting we stop referring to our Gutenberg as the earliest example of printing. They want all our guidebooks corrected, and a whole mess of publications worked on. You'll see." She waited until he had examined the letter, and then asked, "What's the deal? Have they got a case?"

Dr. Wu replied with a broad smile. "Of course. The Chinese and the Japanese and the Koreans were printing books six hundred years before Gutenberg was born."

"Real printing as we know it? Are there examples of it still around?"

"Surely. We have a Buddhist sutra in Japanese right here at the Werner-Bok that was done in 770. The Freer and the Library of Congress have the same thing. They were done for the Empress Shotoku and tradition says she had a million copies printed! We have dozens of volumes here done in the eleven and twelve hundreds."

"Are they real books?"

"Real books. They're even octavo shaped, just like the book of the month. Remember, books were as common in China in the year 1000 as they were in Europe in the 1600s."

"So why do they say Gutenberg invented printing in 1450 or whatever?"

He smiled pleasantly and said, "It is the arrogance of us Westerners. I'm third generation California, myself. So far as we're concerned, anything done in the Far East is on another planet and doesn't count. Real humans only lived in Europe."

"But why aren't the Oriental people screaming bloody murder?"

"They're resigned—and they have the superior side of the argument. The more the West claims, the more superior they feel. But this letter seems to suggest they're not taking it as quietly as they used to."

"Right. So what should we do?"

"Miss Jones, you can fall back on a technicality, if you wish. Since it was easier to create whole pages of the ideographs than many small characters, the early printed books were printed a page at a time like our newspapers and magazines are today. Complete blocks. Gutenberg did invent the idea of making a page out of moveable bits of type. Then, after he'd printed one of his sheets, he'd break the type up, and reassemble it for the next page. If you want to promise the society that in the future you'll be careful to claim only the invention of *moveable* type, you might blunt the argument. For the moment."

"Why for the moment?"

"The Chinese and Japanese used wood block pages. Unfortunately, it seems likely that the Koreans used individual pieces of type from the beginning. We find them in porcelain and in brass before A.D. 1000."

"Why doesn't that shoot down the 'moveable type' promise?"

"Because the specialists are bickering over when and who, and it keeps it from being as neat as Gutenberg."

Crighton looked at the scholar to see if she was being needled. "Are you putting me on?"

Wu smiled. "Sort of. The society has the institution dead to rights, but it hasn't embarrassed anybody here for a hundred years, so I suspect you could stonewall it for a little longer if you wanted to. Seriously, though. I'd suggest you send this letter to the director and recommend that he assemble a committee representing European Studies, Asian Studies, and Science and Technology, and we can all meet and talk about it—endlessly. In the meantime, it will give you something to write back to the Anglo-American Society."

Crighton looked at him closely. "That sounds splendid to me, but I suspect I'm being conned. Is this for real— your solution?"

Wu bowed. "It is. You're one of our favorite people up here, Miss Jones. We would never embarrass you."

"Okay. Consider the paper on its way. Onward and upward with the bureaucracy. You're one of the good guys from my side of the desk, too, Dr. Wu. Bless you thrice over—and your California ancestors, too."

They parted, laughing.

Chapter 3

SHORTLY before five o'clock, Crighton was finishing the last of a half-dozen press releases that would soon be fed into the media stream. The successive pieces would announce a coming exhibition on the invention of the motion picture as an art form, and the releases would be sprayed out at weekly intervals with eight hundred computer-produced mailing labels. The idea was to "build attention" ("there seems to be an awful lot of talk these days about . . .") and as she wrote, her mind caromed off to possible angles that could be used for exclusives for the library's favorite reporters. With the Gutenberg letter still snagged in her mind, she was testing a link ("Edison's invention of the motion picture machine was actually a technological breakthrough just as Gutenberg's was a mechanical one . . . while we think of the book as literary and the motion picture as dramatic, the invention of type and the projection of single frames on a screen first entailed the use of *machines* to be used for other people's words and other people's scenes . . .") when Durance Steele returned.

"Hi, again," Steele said. "Your idea worked beautifully. Mrs. Deane's room will be fine and I've reserved it to start a week from Friday. If you can put up with me till then, it would be marvelous."

"It's done," Crighton replied. "My pleasure." She switched off the lamp and the typewriter and prepared to shut down for the day. "Leave us feed ourselves. What do you taste like? We can go out to something interesting . . . something foreign, or we can walk over to the East Wing and have a quiche among the culture."

"I've never eaten in the museum. That sounds fine. I've parked the car on the Mall, and I presume I can leave it there? This business of parking takes a good deal of the fun out of Washington."

"Yes—and there's no easy solution, either," Crighton said. "It's just as bad here as in New York, but we haven't got New York's taxis to take up the slack. Don't leave anything behind. We'll go straight home after we eat." She turned out the lights and locked the door behind them.

Once on the sidewalk beside the Mall, they turned toward the National Gallery, and Crighton asked, "Do you know Washington?"

"I've been up on a few weekends from Charlottesville, but I've never lived here."

"Where's home?"

"I really don't have one. I was an Army brat and we went from one post to another. My parents split up when I was in high school, and instead of that giving me more places to be from, I moved so frequently I found I wasn't from anywhere. I guess the University of Virginia is my longest stop. I did my undergraduate work there and I've been teaching while I went through the doctorate."

"What program?"

"History."

"Isn't that pretty rare these days?"

15

"Very."

"Have you finished the degree?"

"I've finished the course work and submitted the paper."

Crighton was about to ask, On what? but the complexities of getting into the museum interrupted her thoughts. Ten minutes later she had gotten the two of them into the main gallery, down to the concourse, across the moving sidewalk into the new East Building, up the chromium elevator, and out into the huge atrium of the new gallery.

"I thought it might be fun to eat on the top level. As it gets dark you can see the Capitol out the window and watch everybody on the skywalks in here."

"It is a beautiful building, isn't it?"

"It's a great building, just not much of an art gallery. I find every time they have a show, if they stage it in the old wing I can remember every painting. If they put it in the new side, all I can remember is the room where it was hung. The architecture completely overwhelms the paintings. Let's take that table by the window."

They made small talk and ordered; the food came, and Crighton brought the conversation back to the dissertation. "Is the big discovery you're working on a part of your graduate paper?"

"It turned up in the course of the research, yes." She spoke more deliberately. "If you don't mind, I'd rather not discuss it. I've been rather badly burned with people taking my ideas and claiming they were their own. I've found the academic arena is just one step this side of the drug trade so far as ethics are concerned."

"Ouch. Your cuts sound deep. But once everything's published I assume you'll get the credit you deserve, won't you? Won't your case do its own talking?"

"That is very naive. I had a prof who said that the world was filled with two great fallacies. One was that man was intended to be monogamous, and the other was that

16

right triumphs in the end. Neither was ever true but people have believed them for three thousand years against all evidence to the contrary."

"You don't think that if a thought is really important or a solution really works that it will be recognized? Your Jefferson claimed that if the people really got to hear the issues, they'd always choose the right side."

"You've got to be joking. What gets recognized is what the "proper people" say *can* be recognized. The "ins" flack each other's products. The "outs" could be Shakespeare or Einstein themselves and they'd never even get their stuff read. What's really tragic is the Picassos and the Wyeths and the Rodins and the Calders who're living right now in Indiana and West Virginia who can't even get the attention of their own home town, much less New York or San Francisco."

"Village Hampdens," Crighton said quietly. "What can be done about it?"

"I don't know what they can do with *their* problems, but I sure know what I'm going to do about mine. I've found where the body lies. I've found the closet and I've got the skeletons in it by name, rank, and next of kin."

The woman stopped suddenly and looked out toward the darkening Mall with the museums beginning to glow white across the way. She drew a deep breath and then let it out slowly. "More than anything else, I'm tired. I'm tired of being pushed around. It's an unfair fight—the haves against the have-nots. You can't really break in. The old school tie is just as bad here as they say it is in England. No matter how good you are you can't beat the system—but by God, if I can't beat them, I'll sure as hell see they never forget me."

Crighton looked at her without responding. This bitterness and resentment seemed as out of character as the scholar role had been. Here was a woman who appeared to have it all—intelligence, looks, and apparently money, if her hair and clothing meant anything. The movies would have cast her as the head of a glossy magazine or the producer of a TV series. Something didn't match.

Steele suddenly met Crighton's eyes and went all feminine old-friend charm. "Hey! You know this town, how about letting me drive you around for an hour? You tell me where to go and when to turn and show me the sights. Do you have the time? Postcard Washington. At night. Would you do it? Have you got something you're supposed to do?"

Crighton smiled. "Not a thing. I'd love to. But let's take my car. You look and I'll point and talk."

Later Crighton was to look back on the next two hours as one of the pleasantest evenings she had ever spent. The hard-bitten sophisticate beside her was interested, curious, responsive, and had a fine sense of humor. Ultimately they returned to the Mall and Steele recovered a dark red Porsche and followed Crighton home. As she drove, Crighton brooded. I wonder if the warm friend bit isn't as out of character as the vindictive scholar? I'm missing something here. I wonder what?

Chapter 4

THE following morning Crighton showered and dressed, and as she went to the kitchen to fix breakfast she looked at Durance Steele's closed door and went through the immemorial questions of the hostess. Is she awake? Should I wake her? Should I fix something for her to eat? Leave her a note? Let her sleep? By the time she had reached the tenth permutation, the problem was solved with the appearance of a fully dressed guest, again dramatically made up, hair immaculately in place, stylishly clothed with precise accessories—and wearing a grittily manic expression that seemed to charge the domestic scene.

"Good morning," Steele said. "May I help?"

"Just sit down and enjoy the coffee. If you can tolerate the healthy woman's high-energy breakfast, I'll just double my usual portions. Do you want to ride in with me? I can go past LC and drop you off. No problem."

"No, Crighton. This is an important day for me. I've been working to this for two solid years. This is the payoff. The day the sons-of-bitches get theirs. I'm off for a

19

drive and if I've worked the puzzle right I come back rich and even."

"Hmmm." Crighton decided not to probe. Let her tell the story when she wants to. "So you'll take your own car."

Steele nodded. She sat almost rigidly at the table, her body language clearly signaling the tension and the excitement she felt. Crighton watched her out of the corner of her eye as she worked, thinking there's something unpleasant about the feel of this, and I want no part of it. She thus worked quietly, and it soon became apparent that her guest was lost in her own thoughts as well and felt no need to play the polite role.

They ate in silence, and after an exchange of platitudes, Crighton moved off to work, leaving Steele already on her feet and clearly preparing an immediate departure.

The day did not go well for Crighton. In no time, her own distractions had washed Durance Steele completely from her mind. It was another bomb scare. As she grabbed for her checklist, Crighton thought, How many is this? At least one a month for over four years now, for Christ's sake. If the public knew how frequently the Washington museums and public buildings get these calls, they'd never leave home at all. You'd think by now somebody would know what to do, but it seems like every time one happens, it's the birth of the world all over again. She sprinted for the director's office. Here we go again.

She was right. They were stupidly repetitive. A call would come. "You should know there is a bomb in the Werner-Bok. You've got just fifteen minutes to find it. Death to the tyrant! Life to the People's Party!" Sometimes it would be to revenge the current Third World Caesar. Sometimes it would be some pitiable human being who was savaging back at his tormentors. Sometimes the call would be full of names and organizations; sometimes no identification, no times, no reasons.

This would bring on the "What shall we dos?"—stressful discussions that centered on accents, speech patterns, tone. Is it real or is it a hoax? Down the checklist: one call to the D.C. police; one call to the fire department. Get the head of security. Convene in the director's office—followed by the impossible choices. If you ignore it and it's real, you've jeopardized innocent people. If you clear the building, you burn up the time of scholars who may have traveled thousands of miles for a few hours of access to the treasures. Worse still, you expose the treasures to the chance of smash and grab and fence—or the ultimate horror, grab and hold for ransom. What would you be willing to pay to get the Gettysburg Address back? Columbus's map of the Caribbean? A Gutenberg Bible? And from these cloudland what-ifs comes the inevitable report of five purses stolen from desks while everybody's out on a simple fire drill. Today's version was the individual wronged. Male. Heavily accented. Apparently a genuine accent, but thanks to something (what? television? movies? the Boeing 747?) accents are harder to spot than they used to be. It was wild how an Hispanic accent can sound like Ugandan or maybe Pakistani. You're sure it wasn't Indonesian or Iranian? Especially if the innocent who takes the call goes into perfectly reasonable shock at being the privileged recipient of the telephoned threat.

In any event, they decided *not* to evacuate. The bomb squad came. They did a routine search—and found a very large and very real bomb in the top floor men's room, and the only reason it hadn't gone off was that the perpetrator had failed to set the digital clock for A.M. rather than P.M. It would have blown through every wall in the room and maybe the floor, too. Jesus H. Christ. The sickening feeling of everyone concerned and then the questions. Should we admit it to the press? No. But won't it leak out? Not from us. How about the police? Assurances that the police didn't want publicity any more than the library did. "We get enough copycat crime without the help of television already. Just let us work on who did it—quietly." Finally, by midafternoon, the incident was closed, and everyone went back to their in-boxes, shaken and less sure of themselves than ever. The universal human condition . . . in spades.

The day ground down to its close and Crighton finally laid all the routine tasks aside and sat at her desk, unconsciously returning to the fetal position with her legs pulled up against the desk top and her arms around her knees. She forced herself to think through the day's events and asked again and again, "If we'd known, how would we have played it differently?" Why, you'd have emptied the building into the Mall and left everything right where it was. Millions of dollars worth of rare books and manuscripts and etchings and maps and photographs lying open on every floor? Of course. But how could we have known this one was different when all the others were false alarms? She followed the sequence of events incident by incident but could find no clue. The whole thing was simply a disaster and she felt drained and shrunken.

She finally shook herself free and struggled to her feet. It was well past six and for the first time she thought of Durance Steele, who had presumably returned from her climactic day. She wondered casually if she'd find her triumphant or crushed.

She drove home to discover a dark apartment. No sign of Steele at all. She had given her a key, hadn't she? Yes, no doubt of it. For the first time, Crighton felt a trace of irresolution about her guest. I wonder what did happen? she thought. Is she hanging one on in celebration or getting stoned numb out of disappointment? In any event, the odds were there was no sense of waiting supper, so she put some soup in the microwave and pulled together what looked like a smugly healthful salad.

Having finished her meal, she slumped down on the

couch to watch the end of an ancient "M*A*S*H"—and slid straight into an emotionally exhausted sleep.

Three hours later she was lifted back into consciousness by what appeared to have been an endlessly ringing telephone. She lurched to her feet and staggered to the receiver. She lifted it and said, "Ummm?"

A woman speaking very clearly said, "You snatch-licking bitch, you think you've won. Don't fool yourself. You've killed yourself. You are as good as dead. Dead, as in your pretty blood all over those round boobs of yours. Are you hearing me, pretty thing? You are dead. Quite dead. Very dead. Completely dead . . ."

The phone went smoothly into a dial tone. For no particular reason, Crighton thought, They pushed the button down . . . why didn't they slam the receiver? The incongruity of the situation began to hit her as she became fully awake. She found, oddly, that she felt no particular fear or threat. There was no sense that the person was talking to *her*. Jesus, she thought, I've just had my first obscene phone call. But no, obscene phone calls come from men. That was a woman. And that wasn't meant for me. Who did they think I was?

Suddenly she was quite awake. "You think you've won." It must have something to do with Durance's *grand coup*. Apparently she'd brought it off, whatever it was, and it appeared to have elicited just about the fury she'd wanted.

Crighton walked to the kitchen and began to brew a pot of coffee while dredging for the conversation in her memory. A woman with a slight Southern accent. Not Mississippi or Alabama. Just soft. Virginia or Eastern Shore Maryland. Low, throaty, cultured. No hysteria—and no real anger. Controlled. Oh, Christ, I'm back at that bomb scare looking for accents. And how scared should I be? If it's just words, there's no reason to get up-tight about it—in fact, that's probably exactly what she was hoping for.

23

She'll love it. But what if it's real? What if someone really is going to spill her blood down her front? Oh, God, this is ridiculous. Where is the woman? She'd better get here soon—and be sober enough to deal with this. I'm sure as hell not up to it at this hour of the night.

Crighton sat down at the table and deliberately drank two cups of very hot, very black coffee—and five minutes later went straight to sleep with her forehead on her arms. At three o'clock discomfort lifted her sufficiently to drive her to the couch, where she slept, fully dressed, straight on until morning.

Chapter 5

Aт seven o'clock Thursday morning, Crighton re-joined the human race. She awoke slowly, she was stiff and sore, and her face felt like she'd been sleeping face down in sand, but she was functioning. She dragged her-self to the bathroom and threw handfuls of cold water against her cheeks and forehead, and the cooling flood brought blood back and cleared her head. She walked back into the living room, gradually seizing the offensive. All right, she told herself, let's see where we stand.

The first question was, Had Durance Steele come in during the night? A quick check of her bedroom and the kitchen answered that one. No. Her bed was smoothly made and untouched. Her clothes were in the closet, her makeup in a case on the dresser. There was a red leather briefcase on the floor and an AAA map on the bedspread. Everything else was untouched.

Crighton returned to the kitchen and sat down in a hard chair. She'd had enough of overstuffed cushions for a while. The residue of the night's coffee sat before her, and it struck her that fresh caffeine might be a good idea, so she got up and started a new potful. Now what?

That damn phone call. She was going to have to face up to doing something about it. Presumably the first order of business was to see that Durance Steele got the message so either it could be dismissed or she could protect herself against whatever it meant. How to find Steele and tell her?

The only link Crighton had with her short-term guest was the woman at the Library of Congress, Lynda Claasson. Too early to call anyone. She'd better use the time getting dressed for the day; what she had on looked like it had been in the back of a truck for the winter.

An hour later she had showered, redressed, and had had the usual energy-up breakfast. There was nothing in the mailbox downstairs, and still no sign of Steele. Although the Library of Congress did not open to the public until nine, the staff reported at eight-thirty, so within minutes she was able to place her call.

"Lynda! Thank heavens you're there," she saluted her when she came on. "Do you remember that Durance Steele woman you sent me a couple of days ago? Right. Looking for a room. Well, I found a spot for her for next week, but I put her up here with me in the meantime, and I'm desperately trying to find her. She was supposed to come home last night and she never made it. She's had an emergency phone call and I don't know where she is to give it to her." Crighton had long since decided to blur what the call was about. She could think of no way of euphemizing the threat without sounding like an utter fool. "Do you have her address or phone or something?"

"No problem," Claasson replied. "She had to fill out her pedigree to get to use the manuscripts. Wait a minute. I'll copy it off the register." Claasson was back in a few moments with the information and Crighton transcribed it.

"You haven't seen her at LC, have you?" Crighton asked.

"Not since I pointed her your way day before yesterday."

"Did she tell you what she was looking for?"

"Sort of. She implied she had a major piece of revisionism about Jefferson and the War of 1812 and something else. The main thing I recall was something about how it was going to blow my skirts over my head. I was somewhat surprised at the chauvinist image—particularly since I was wearing slacks at the time."

"Did she mean that what she'd discovered would affect *you* or just that you'd be surprised?"

"Hmmm. I think I assumed the latter, but I don't remember exactly what she said at this late date."

"Okay! You've done good. I'll take it from here. If she shows up, for heaven's sake have her get in touch with me—either here or at the Werner-Bok."

They parted and without shifting Crighton dialed the number she'd been given. In a short time she had established that, one, it was a dormitory at the University of Virginia; two, that Durance Steele had moved out two weeks before; and three, that the forwarding address she had left behind was the same as the one she'd used as a home address as an undergraduate. Crighton got the telephone number there and with astonishing speed found herself talking to a military police post at Camp Jackson that had been deactivated three years before. There was no one living on the base except the MP security company and none of them was named Steele.

Crighton felt like she'd hit the dead end signal in a video game.

A quick call to Mrs. Deane on Capitol Hill confirmed her assumption that Steele had not gone to her reserved room a week early. To Crighton's frustration, she realized that she had exhausted every point of touch she knew about Durance Steele.

Now what?

A few minutes of intense concentration convinced her that, reluctant as she was to admit it, she needed reinforcements. When she needed to reach out and touch someone, she'd found a hug from Steve Carson the most reassuring, and although in ordinary circumstances he was the last person she'd let know she needed help, she did now, and this was no time to stand on pride. Carson had been at Williamsburg since he'd gotten his doctorate, helping with the excavation of the Davenport Hundred. It was still early enough that he might not have left for the site. She hurriedly found his number, called, and to her immense relief, he answered.

"Carson," she said, "I need you."

"Don't move. I'm on my way. You've decided to marry me. Shall I bring a parson or have you got one waiting?"

"Shut up, you nut. This is even worse than the thought of being stuck with you for a lifetime. I have got myself into a weird piece of confusion, and it's just barely possible I could use some advice. Have you got long enough to listen?"

"Woman, you know I could hang on your words for the rest of my life. Bathe me with the soft sounds of your voice."

"Jesus. Just stay quiet. Here's what's happened." She gave him a crisp but detailed report of the events of the past two days, omitting nothing that she could think of. She ended somewhat breathlessly with, "And that's where we stand. Have you got some brilliant suggestion as to what I should do next?"

Rather to her surprise, he responded quite seriously. "Yeah, woman, you've got yourself a real one this time. Wait a minute, let me think." There was a pause, and he said, "Okay, here's some random. The first thing you should do is call the Alderman Library at U. Va. and ask for Landon Culliver. Landon is one of the great cocksmen of the Old South, and pictures himself as the last of the cavaliers, but he knows everybody and everything. He's a marvelous gossip. Very useful."

"How old is he?"

"Our age, but he's senescing fast. Give him a call—feel free to drop my name—and tell him you're trying to find Steele. For God's sake don't say why—just ask him if he's ever heard of her or who would know where she is. If Steele really was a history major, she'd have to live in Alderman, and Culliver would know her. His own paper was an outrageous attempt to prove that the F.F.V. were a triumph of selective breeding. He even did stud lines as an appendix. No one ever knew whether he meant it or if it was a colossal put-on. Marvelous. They gave him the Ph.D. just to keep him quiet."

"Got it. Anything else?"

"Yeah. I sympathize with you over that death threat thing. Surely it's just a bluff . . . intimidation . . . but probably you ought to tell someone—the problem is, if it's just a con, Steele would be horribly embarrassed if the authorities got involved, but if it isn't, you could be pretty responsible. Why don't you call Lieutenant Conrad and do the just-between-you-and-me bit and ask him if it would be all right not to panic until we know something firm. Does this make sense?"

"Perfectly. Carson, I'd say I was deeply in your debt if I wasn't afraid of how you'd try to collect. But bless you, Stephen. You are a good thing. Just don't let it go to your head."

Instead of his usual hyperbole, he replied, "I feel for you, C. Jones. For God's sake, call me this evening and tell me how it all came out. Now go call Culliver. If he tries to take advantage of your innocence, tell him you belong to me."

29

"I do not belong . . . oh, go away. But thanks, you bum." She was calling the Charlottesville operator for a number within seconds.

In no time she had Landon Culliver on the line. He sounded exactly like she had expected, laid back, arch, and with a carefully preserved Virginia accent. She fed him the questions as instructed, and he rose to them like Raleigh meeting the Queen. "Why, Miss Jones, I do indeed know your Durance Steele. Great heavens, yes! She was our favorite scandal. She and her roommate made last semester bearable. My goodness, yes."

"The roommate . . . uh, he or she? Are we talking female?"

"Oh, God, yes. Gloriously female! A stunning woman. The two roomed together for two or three years while they were doing their graduate work. The roommate is a creamy Southern type, an example of our aristocracy at its superlative best. They were both taking courses and trying to pick a topic and they absolutely energized our social scene. They frequently double dated and oh my God, my dear, when they'd hit a room it was heart-stopping.

"All went like a thirties movie until suddenly La Roommate fell for a guy and moved out—and I'm sorry to say, your friend Steele simply came apart at the seams. Apparently there had been more to the relationship than anyone had suspected. Well! The two had shared a carrell here at Alderman and it seemed that before La Roommate fled, Steele had Xeroxed great quantities of Roommate's notes and her research material and before anyone realized what had happened, Steele had taken her topic and got it certified by the Grad Board, and then written it. Dear God, yes, it was a complete and total rip-off! Roommate blew sky-high and took her case to the Grad Board and it's to be adjudicated any day now."

Crighton had the sensation of the room beginning to

turn slowly to the right. "But . . . but," she said, "if the roommate had chosen a topic, how could Steele steal it?"

"Roommate never had it certified. She kept agonizing over it and talking to advisors and changing her mind and adjusting the parameters—and she'd never set the hard edges and gotten it recorded."

"But won't the board find for her anyway? Simple equity or justice or fair play or something?"

"Ah, my dear, it's not that simple. Madame Steele has produced a thesis. Written the words. From one point of view, she's done the work; her roommate only talked about it."

"But the roommate had all the research to prove that she'd been working on it—"

"That might be useful, but it's beside the point, Miss Jones. The consensus in the lounge and bar is that your friend Steele's paper will be disallowed and she'll be censured and thrown out—really ruined professionally. Not because of what she did but who she is."

"Who is she?"

"Nobody. Roommate is F.F.V."

"That's the second time I've heard those letters."

"Yes, indeed. First Families of Virginia. The local version of 'came over on the Mayflower.' And the board is F.F.V. six to three. Some of those names have been on it since Mr. Jefferson's time."

"Would they really vote class?"

"Would an Adams expel a Saltonstall? For that matter, would a Conant expel a Kennedy? Remember, they have to live with mommy and daddy—it's not the kids that are the problem. They'll be meeting the old folks in parish house, board room, and club. What could they possibly say over drinks if they'd done the dirty to their little girl?"

"Oh, Lord," Crighton sighed. She thought, But the

31

Southern voice had said, "You won." "Mr. Culliver, are you sure the case hasn't been decided yet?"

"It might well have been. The board met on Saturday so the off-campus types could come in. The decisions go out promptly, but they go to the affected parties first and then to the public—read that 'media'—three days later. If your friend Steele has gotten her mail, she should know by now." Crighton thought, Gotten her mail where? Camp Jackson? She said, "And there's no talk on campus?"

"We are standing on tippy-toe trying to catch the first whisper, but there is not a sound as yet."

"Wow! You've opened a whole new scene to me, Mr. Culliver. I don't know what to do next, but you've certainly extended the possibilities. By the way, what's the roommate been doing since the excitement?"

"She's disappeared completely. Rumor has it daddy got her a government job and she's melted into the faceless mass. We trust that the board's ruling will flush her out one way or another. God, she was an ornament to the campus here."

Crighton had the feeling of wanting to press down hard on the top of her head, but she said, "Well! This has certainly been helpful. I'll tell Steve Carson how wonderful you've been. I can't thank you enough."

"My dear, the Cardinal Society is having a little soirée at the end of the month, and I wonder if you would enhance my standing among my peers by joining me for the occasion? Some of these affairs prove to be—"

"Thank you very, very much, but I'm expecting to be in Beijing that weekend, but the next time I'm in Charlottesville, I hope you'll let me look you up. You really have been so very kind." She continued to talk as she delicately pressed down on the phone button.

Chapter 6

"**G**ODDAMMIT," said Crighton Jones. "This has gone on long enough. We go through that room with a fine-toothed comb." She stood up abruptly and turned and then hesitated. Better warn the bureaucracy. She dialed the Werner-Bok Library quickly, and in the absence of the director himself told his secretary that a personal crisis had developed and she would be in late. With that she marched to the bedroom, where Durance Steele's makeup case was the first thing that caught her eye.

Crighton walked to it and methodically emptied it onto the dresser. There was no name, no address, no prescription with doctor or pharmacy, no notation, no identifying marks of any kind. She then went to the closet and brought out each piece of clothing and laid it across the bedspread. Again, pocket by pocket, label by label, she went through all the pieces. As she had expected, the array of name stores was dramatic—New York, Dallas, San Francisco—the woman had either been around a great deal or was wild about catalogs. Designers' names appeared in a full third of the ensembles, but again, nothing that would expand on her knowledge of the whereabouts of Durance Steele. There was an owner's tag on the empty suitcase in the closet, but it carried only the address of her Charlottesville dormitory, and that was no longer news. As Crighton turned back to stare at the array now spread across bed and dresser, she noted the red leather briefcase, half hidden beside a wastebasket.

She lunged for it and opened it on the bedspread. It was quite empty except for a pair of tired pieces of paper each a part of a different, Xeroxed sheet. Both sheets appeared to have been copied from the same government document, which had the words "13th Congress. No. 371. 3d Session." printed across the top. The two pages appeared well handled and much used. Recalling Landon Culliver's story, she could picture their having come from research material assembled at least a year before. She read them closely. The first said,

BOOKS AND PAPERS OF THE HOUSE OF
REPRESENTATIVES
AND THE LIBRARY OF CONGRESS
LOST BY THE CONFLAGRATION OF THE
CAPITOL IN 1814
COMMUNICATED TO THE HOUSE OF
REPRESENTATIVES, SEPTEMBER 22, 1814

SIR: CITY OF WASHINGTON, *September* 15, 1814

In order to correct any erroneous statements or representations which may go, or have gone out to the public, in relation to the destruction of your office, we deem it our duty to make the following statement of facts: At the time you left the city, (which was in the latter part of the month of July,) for the springs in Virginia and Pennsylvania, for the recovery of your health, all was quiet, and we believe no fears were entertained for the Chesapeake, and what was seen in the newspapers, of troops being ordered from Europe to America.

About the middle of August it was stated that the enemy was in the bay, in great force, and, on the 19th of that month, the whole body of the militia of the District of Columbia was called out, under which call every clerk of the office was taken into the field, except Mr. Frost, and marched to meet the enemy.

On the 21st, the first of the undersigned clerks was furloughed, by Brigadier General Smith, at the request of Colonel George Magruder, for the purpose of returning to the city, to take care of, and save such part of the books and papers of the clerk's office, as he might be able to effect, in case the enemy should get possession of the place; he arrived here in the night of that day.

His orders from Colonel George Magruder were, not to begin packing up until it was ascertained that the clerks at the War Office were engaged in that business; and it was not until 12 o'clock, on Monday, the 22nd, that we were informed that they had begun to move the effects of that office, although we were subsequently told that it had commenced the day before.

We immediately went to pack up, and Mr. Burch went out in search of wagons or other carriages, for the transportation of the books and papers; every wagon, and almost every cart, belonging to the city, had been previously impressed into the service of the United States, for the transportation of the baggage of the army; the few he was able to find were loaded with the private effects of individuals, who were moving without the city; those he attempted to hire, but, not succeeding, he claimed a right to impress them; but, having no legal authority, or military force to aid him, he, of course, did not succeed. He then sent off three messengers into the country, one of whom obtained from Mr. John Wilson, whose residence is six miles from the city, the use of a cart and four oxen; it did not arrive at the office, until after dark on Monday night, when it was immediately laden with the most valuable records and papers, which were taken, on the same night, nine miles, to a safe and secret place in the country. We

35

continued to remove as many of the most valuable books and papers, having removed the manuscript records, as we were able to do with our one cart, until the morning of the day of the battle of Bladensburg, after which we were unable to take away any thing further.

The second sheet appeared to be the conclusion of the same letter:

We regret very much the loss of your private accounts and vouchers, amongst which, we are sorry to add, were the receipts and accounts of the expenditures of the contingent moneys of the House of Representatives; they were in the private drawer of Mr. George Magruder, which being locked, and the key not in our possession, we delayed to break it open until the last extremity, after which it escaped our recollection.

It is well known to one of us (Mr. Burch,) that the receipts were from the first of January last, and embraced nearly the whole amount of the appropriation for the contingent expenses of the House.

A number of the printed books were also consumed, but they were all duplicates of those which have been preserved.

We have thus given you a full account of our proceedings during the troublesome scene, and we flatter ourselves you will not see in them any thing to disapprove, as we were guided solely by a zealous endeavor to discharge our duty to you, and to the public.

S. BURCH
To PATRICK MAGRUDER, Esq.   J.T. FROST
Clerk to the House of Representatives

A faded streak of yellow highlighter ran the length of the phrase, "but they were all duplicates of those which have been preserved."

Crighton held a sheet in each hand and thought, could

this be the big deal she was all excited about, or were these simply two pieces of trash that were left over after she took the important stuff with her? They seemed to be from the right time period, but they certainly lacked the drama that had been promised.

The letter clearly related to the Library of Congress, so she concluded she'd best read it to someone up there and get a second opinion. No, might as well take the Xeroxes themselves and show them to somebody. But show them to whom? Lynda Claasson might know. She returned to the telephone and dialed the lady, who was both in and promising to stay that way. Crighton promised she would be right up. With the rush hour over, Crighton was able to circle the Mall and arrived at the Library of Congress in barely thirty minutes, considerably faster than if she'd tried it an hour earlier. She went straight to Claasson's office in the Manuscripts Division.

"So here it is," Crighton said after having reported a good deal more of the situation than she had shared in her original conversation. "Are these things telling us anything we don't already know? What do they mean—if anything?"

Claasson read the pages with an increasing frown, and responded slowly, "Hmmm. I've never heard of any of this. This is quite strange, and if it's real, it could very well be what Steele meant when she promised our skirts over our heads. Let me give you the background.

"The Library of Congress, you recall, is based on the private collection of Thomas Jefferson. What happened is that during the early days of the government, Congress borrowed books from the private libraries in New York and Philadelphia for its own use, but when it moved to the District of Columbia in 1800, they started buying their own books—accumulating the Library of Congress—Congress's library. The Founding Fathers had managed to collect about three thousand volumes by the War of 1812,

37

when the British stormed into town and set fire to the Capitol and the White House and wiped out Ye Embryonic Library of C. to the last book. Apparently everyone was horrified at the time, and for some reason there was more hue and cry over the burning of the books than there was over the loss of the building. Thomas Jefferson heard about it in Monticello and generously offered his own personal library to replace it. The Congress took him up on it, and all six or seven thousand volumes were moved up here, so Congress was back in the library business very quickly after the fire. What we at LC always point out is that this is the reason for the extraordinarily broad subject collection in what would normally be just a narrow, legislative library. What with Jefferson being a patriot and a diplomat and a secretary of state and a president, he'd assembled the largest library in America and the one with the broadest sweep of subjects. Remember, he was big on science and architecture and foreign culture—the whole schmeir. Congress recognized what hot stuff it was, so it immediately began adding to it in all the categories. The result is that we've got the largest library in the world now, and from the very beginning it was getting practically anything of importance on everything from anywhere."

Crighton was following intently. "So what's the significance of these things?" She pointed to the two Xeroxed sheets.

"Well, these would appear to relate to the three thousand *original* books. The prefire stuff. I'd always heard that they didn't have time to save any of the volumes and they'd burned up right on their shelves. This seems to imply that the books were actually moved out of Washington and weren't burned at all. If this were so, you've got a whole mess of unanswered questions. What happened to them afterwards? Do they still exist? If so, where? They certainly aren't in the Library of Congress now. And remember, you'd be talking about shelves and shelves of books—most of them first editions now two hundred years old! Also, it puts a slight film over the antecedents of this great institution. If they didn't *have* to replace the original books, it makes it look like someone faked the loss just to slip one great chunk of money to my hero—I'm a Jeffersonian myself. I think it was true that the price they paid him was *very* generous. The small-minded could perceive this as playing around with 'the people's' money. Presumably Jefferson really thought the collection had burned and he thought he was doing a good thing, but did everybody in Congress think so? If *anybody* knew the collection was still intact, why did they all vote Jefferson the cash? Come to think about it, I seem to recall that they just barely did. Daniel Webster was against it, I remember. In fact, I think almost all of the yes votes came from the South—the votes that approved the appropriation. No, Crighton, if these pages are real, they do open up a number of interesting possibilities."

"I think I'm sorry I asked!" She grimaced. "But seriously, this is exactly what I needed to know. You've told me that this may actually be what Steele was doing in Washington. Given this 'discovery,' what would she be doing at LC?"

"That's a bit hard to say. First, checking to see if the documents were genuine, I suppose."

"No," Crighton said, "I think we can assume she had pretty much validated that in the past year, from the way she talked—at least she'd convinced herself that whatever she'd found was the McCoy."

"Then the next thing," Claasson continued, "could well be the pursuit of 'Whatever happened to the original books?'"

"What would there be here now that would help answer that?"

"Oh, you could go through contemporary letters to see

if any of the guys who voted for buying the Jefferson books discussed it in their weekly letter home to their wives. Or you could go down to the Maps Division and get contemporary maps to see what lay on roads nine miles into Maryland." Crighton thought of the Maryland road map lying on the bedspread.

"Would it be possible to check to see if Steele was using any maps the day she came up here?"

"Sure, let me call down and have them look at their sign-in sheets." Claasson placed the call without having to look up the number, and after a pair of questions reported, "Bingo! She was there and working in the Early American section."

"Oh, God. The more I learn the worse I feel. Bless your heart. You have been a gold mine, and certainly have saved an enormous amount of time. You may have saved a life, too, before we're finished with this. I think I'll go back to the Werner-Bok and try to sort this all out. If you get any further ideas, for heaven's sake call me. I need all the help I can get."

They exchanged reassurances and Crighton headed for the street and the Werner-Bok Library.

Once back at her desk, she called the director's office and reported in, then quickly placed a call to Lieutenant Conrad, her usual contact with the District Police Department. Conrad was across the Anacostia sweating out a hostage situation—a husband was holding his wife and her boy friend at gun point—but they would have him call Crighton as soon as he returned to the office.

With these obligations met, she checked her calendar to see what was on for the day. Appointments at hourly intervals. Ten o'clock: WRRT television coming to check out coverage of the cowboy show. Eleven o'clock: delegation from the Denver Art Museum to work out negotiations for borrowing Zebulon Pike materials and working sketches from the Remington and Catlin collections.

40

Three o'clock: art book publisher to talk about arrangements to photograph the Saint Sophia mosaic studies. She had started to call the various curators involved to be sure they remembered the times, when the phone rang under her hand. She picked it up; it was Steve Carson from Williamsburg.

"Crighton? Good. I couldn't stand it. My curiosity has got me so distracted I dug through two deposition layers without measuring either one. I'm a menace to archeology. What's happening?"

"Bless you for calling, friend. I'm running four ways at once. I've got things going here at the library that I can't shut down, but I'm scared silly I ought to be doing something about the Steele business. Let me bring you up to date." She reported her expedition to the Library of Congress and said, "So that's where I seem to stand. Here's some worst-case speculation: if my Southern caller was the roommate, as seems all too likely, she would probably be in a murderous condition even if she was completely sane. Steele has taken her idea, she's preempted her dissertation topic, and she's getting away with it—with the officials' blessing. She'll even have the doctorate come commencement, and roommate comes out of it with absolutely nothing. She can't even use her own research—the topic's been done now. If she's brooded about it, and maybe about their earlier relationship, she could have flipped clear out and she could really be a floating menace. She could very well intend to cut her pretty throat—literally! As I see it, and never mind what the justice of the situation might be, I've got to find Steele and warn her," Crighton concluded. "But where the hell is she? The last I heard she was going out to complete something—she said something like 'If I've solved the puzzle right, I'll be back rich and even.' So what did she go out to do?"

"I agree with you all the way, woman," Carson said. "I

think Magnolia is indeed closing in, and either she's already found her and that's why Steele hasn't showed up, or Magnolia's as frustrated as you are, and Steele's not coming back may have saved her life. But it could well be a race to see if we can get her warned before Magnolia gets there first."

"Bless you for the 'we,' Carson."

"Oh, hell, I'm useless here till we get this resolved. Useless? I'm a menace! I'll be right up. I can make it in three hours; maybe less. But there's a couple of things you might do while I'm in transit, if you want to. It'll speed things up. Under the heading of 'What did she go out to do?' how does this grab you? We have to assume that Steele believed that what was in those photocopies was true. That means she knows what happened to the original collection of the Library of Congress—three thousand first editions worth thousands in their own time. You think she said she'd be coming back rich. So how could she capitalize on that kind of antique knowledge? I can think of two ways: If she just knows who kept the books in the first place and has found some well-born (and well-heeled) relative, she can threaten to embarrass them publicly and is charging them to keep quiet. That's assuming the collection has long since been dissipated. But if she thinks they're still all together somewhere, and she thinks she's found them, then she's really got somebody by the short hair. She can either threaten to make a big stink over the theft and historic graft and corruption, or she can insist that she get cut in and start selling the things off. How do you read the I'll-have-gotten-even bit?"

"Well," Crighton answered, "you and that Culliver character keep waving the F.F.V. over me. If the books are in the hands of some of your great Southern names, it would be a real embarrassment to the family. If one of my kin had stolen three thousand books before they ran off to Oklahoma, we'd all brag about it, but I presume if I was

F.F.V. it might not be so funny. Are many of the names still around?"

"Hell, yes. We've got Byrds and Carters and Randolphs and Tylers all over the place. Most of them are Episcopalians and all of them are in politics. No, they wouldn't find this sort of thing as funny as you do on the frontier."

"Well, until we think of something better, that's probably what Steele is up to. Either she's going to get her cut of the books and get rich, or she's going to tell all and get even. Either way we sure as hell need to know where she thinks the books are."

"It's thin," Carson said, "but it's the best we've got so far. You put it as an either/or. I think as you originally reported it, Steele said 'and'—rich *and* even, but that's a detail. This is the best we've got now. Let's do a crash job trying to figure out where she must have gone yesterday morning."

"You mean duplicate Steele's research and break her 'puzzle' ourselves?"

"You got any better idea?"

Crighton sighed. "No, but it seems just a tad hopeless with the roommate circling around like an avenging angel. Steele spent a couple of years on it."

"Nonsense, woman! She must have wasted lots of time trying to find out if it was real. We skip that and go straight through on the assumption that it's not 'if' but 'where.' Got a pencil? Let me give you a shopping list."

Crighton said, "Ready. Lay it on me."

"Okay. Get a good biography of Jefferson—Dumas Malone's probably the best—and get a history of the Library of Congress. Take Steele's photocopies up to your Serials Division and wave 'em at somebody in the government documents section and ask if they can tell where they came from. If they can, get the whole book they're in so we can see if there's anything that came before or after that we should know. Then see if you can get your

43

friend Claasson to make a couple more calls to see where else Steele may have been digging up there. You know she was looking at maps, and she must have been doing manuscripts, if that's where she started. See if Claasson will tell you which collections she'd checked out. Manuscripts types keep who-used-what records forever in case something turns up missing a decade later. Can you think of anything else?"

"Whoosh," said Crighton. "This'll keep me busy enough. We can make wider sweeps when you get here. Do you want to come here to the office or do you want to go right to the apartment?"

"My love, this is not the time to renew that discussion. You recall, I have suggested on other occasions that it might be useful for me to have a key to your bedroom . . . house, that is. You never yielded, and now see how right I was? Will you never trust me?"

"Creep."

"She loves me. It's all I ask of life. I'll be there mid-afternoon. Keep the faith."

"Carson, bless you. Come carefully."

At two o'clock on Thursday afternoon, Carson sailed into Crighton's basement office.

"My God, woman," he said, "you are always more beautiful than I can remember. Magnificent design. Everything in just the right place and perfectly proportioned. I am very fond of you."

Crighton shook her head and said, "How many times do I have to tell you we are no longer flattered by your views on our physical characteristics? If you want to make points these days, you've got to salute our intelligence, our style, our talent—"

Carson went around the desk and kissed her firmly and in detail.

"I must admit," Crighton said when she got her breath back, "I do enjoy that. You do it very well."

"Only because you inspire me so. There's much more where that came from, by the way. Suitably recharged, I am now prepared to work!" He threw his jacket over a filing case and said, "Did you get the stuff? Anything new from Steele?"

"I did. There it is on the table. You can work right there, if you want to. You didn't tell me Dumas came in six volumes. I could have slipped a disc. Steele's documents are from the very official *State Papers of the United States*. I've got the right volume, but I didn't have time to look inside. And no, nothing from Steele. I've called the apartment regularly, and it just rings. I've got to go up and prep some Byzantine specialists, so I'll leave you. Good hunting." She ran her hand across his cheek and into his hair. "And I'm very glad you're here, though I'll never tell you." She rushed out the door, clutching clipboard and notebooks.

By the end of the day, Carson had made great strides with his printed materials. Crighton had come in and out, but the two had only waved at each other in silence. Not until five o'clock did they break the cadence of their activities and prepare for a conference. Crighton slipped off her shoes and sat on her stockinged feet, and Carson spun his chair around from the table and slid down on his heels.

"So where do we stand?" Crighton asked. "Find anything?"

"Found lots," he said. "We're much farther down the road. To wit. First, the photocopies are the whole story, almost. There's nothing that relates to the library before them—the documents are printed in chronological order— but there are two big ones not too much later than Steele's copied one. According to Steele's piece, on September 15

45

the clerks say, 'A number of the printed books were consumed but they were all duplicates of those which have been preserved.' On December 12 comes a new report in which a committee on the loss of the Capitol reports that they, and I quote, 'have satisfactory evidence that the library of Congress consisting of volumes agreeably to the catalogue herewith submitted was destroyed by the enemy of the 24th of August last.' This fries the hell out of the two library clerks, and on December 17 the clerks say officially, in writing, in the *State Papers of the United States,* 'the several loads which were saved, were taken from the shelves on which they were placed, and deposited in the carts by which they were taken away; they have suffered no injury, and, to have procured boxes or trunks to pack them in, if that plan had been preferred, would have been utterly impossible.'

"That's it," Carson concluded. "No further mention of anything in the official *State Papers.* On September 15 the clerks are saying they got an ox cart and took the stuff nine miles out of town. On December 12, the Congress is saying the library was destroyed. On December 17, the clerks say it suffered no injury. Very strange indeed. At first glance you've only got two explanations: either the clerks were lying in their teeth to protect their tails—forgive the metaphor—or the official committee is lying in its teeth in order to give T. Jefferson umpteen thousand dollars of the taxpayers' money for a bunch of books it didn't really need."

"There's got to be some other choice," Crighton said.

"Let's hope so. But that brings us directly to Dumas Malone. He's got a lot of good stuff about Jefferson's generous offer and the sale and moving the books up from Monticello that we'll want to study a syllable at a time, but there are a few high spots. First, he makes no reference whatsoever to the possibility that the books weren't completely burned. *But,* he certainly provides a possible motive. He says Jefferson was in terrible fiscal straits. He'd mortgaged everything around the homestead, he'd underwritten a bunch of other people's loans and they'd gone bad leaving him liable, and he had personal debts going back for years. According to Malone, two-thirds of the money he ultimately got from selling the books went right through his hands to his creditors. Would you believe," Carson opened a volume at an inserted waste card, "four thousand eight hundred seventy dollars of it went straight to Thaddeus Kosciuszko, the Polish patriot, to pay off a long-standing. The venerable K. must have been astonished at that late date."

"How much did they pay Jefferson for the books?"

Carson searched and replied, "Twenty-three thousand nine hundred fifty dollars. I brooded on that. That was a fairly tidy sum in those days. A skilled carpenter or a blacksmith made about three hundred dollars a year. That's three hundred, not three thousand. Government clerks were paid a dollar a day, too, so if you use that as a yardstick, you get an equivalent of well over one hundred dollars per *volume* in today's money. Very generous for some slightly used books.

"Malone gives us another fat bonus, too. He provides some juicy details on how they moved Jefferson's books up from Monticello that we can use in trying to figure out where Steele's hidden collection might have been put."

Carson pulled a spiral notebook toward him and read from his penciled notes. "Given: we're told that the LC collection was taken nine miles out of Washington by ox cart—and a pretty damn big cart, too, apparently—it took four oxes to pull it."

"Oxen."

"What? Yeah. Malone says Jefferson's collection came up from Charlottesville in ten horse-drawn wagons, and it took six days to do it. We know the Jefferson collection had six thousand five hundred books in it, so there must

47

have been six hundred fifty books per wagon. Therefore you can move six hundred fifty books in a day, but we'll need a map to find out how far. Now, the original LC collection had three thousand volumes in it, and the ox cart could easily have been large enough to have held nearly a thousand volumes a load. The clerks said they made 'several' trips. If several equaled only three, they could have moved the whole thing. Hell, you could have moved all three thousand in just five horse wagons, so all we have to do is to make a few calculations of time and distance, and we're in business."

Crighton laughed sardonically. "Are we indeed? You're sure you're really getting closer to the truth with all this stuff?"

Carson grimaced. "You know, that thought has occurred to me, too, but no, I think if you work on it, we can do two things with considerable validity. One: get a map and see what places are still standing in Maryland, nine miles from the Capitol building. A simple kid's compass will give us the arc. And then, two: figure out how far a wagon can go in a day and draw that arc around Washington, and see how many 1812 buildings are still standing—buildings that'd be big enough to house three thousand books."

"An arc and a map? Carson, you are stripping your gears. That's an enormous leap from what ought to be to what is. There're too many other things that could have happened to those books a hundred and fifty years ago."

"Not as many as you'd think—I'll explain later—but I would have loved to try it on Dumas Malone himself to see what he would've said. Even more, I'd love to know what he thought about the possibility that the original collection was not burned and still exists. Unfortunately, the great man is no longer with us, but I think most of his research team is still at U. Va. Dammit, I don't know any of them, and I'm afraid if I called them out of the blue, they'd think the lunatic fringe had broken loose. I wish Edward George were here. He'd either know them, or he could drop names that would give him some standing with them. Do you have any idea where our beloved mentor is?"

"I haven't heard from him since Christmas. He sent me a card from New Haven with the Yale Library on it," Crighton said. She laughed. "I've been using the cutline off it regularly. It showed a sign out in front of the Sterling, and the sign said, THIS IS NOT THE STERLING LIBRARY . . . THE LIBRARY IS INSIDE. Love it! I think it's usually credited to Rudy Rogers, the librarian there. But you're so right. We do have need of him and now. Why don't you call him and at least get him to phone the Malone people for us?"

Carson thought a moment, and said, "I'll do it. I'd like to try some options on him, too, while I'm at it. We don't have much time to go down too many dead ends. He could give us some feeling of what's valider than what isn't."

"So come on," Crighton said. "Let's shut down here and call him from the apartment. I don't want to put anything on the company phone bill."

"Have you got an extension so we can both listen in?"

"I do. There's one in the bedroom."

"Then let's go. My car's in a lot on F Street, but you wait for me in the lobby when you get home. We know Magnolia knows the telephone number, but we don't know if she knows where the phone is located. I want to be sure she hasn't got the door mined."

Crighton smothered a smart remark as they parted. He just might, she thought, be right.

When Carson arrived at her apartment house, he found her waiting in the lobby, as instructed.

Crighton said, "Well, we've got one of our questions

answered." She handed him a greeting card addressed to Durance Steele with Crighton's address typed on the envelope. Postmark: District of Columbia.

"I opened it. I figured what the hell. I thought there might be some kind of a name or address we could work from."

Carson extracted the folded card. It was a charming drawing of a little girl, beribboned and winsome, looking straight out at the reader. Above her were the words, "Missing you." Inside was the same girl being kissed on the cheek by a second. Whatever caption had originally been there was now covered with a typed label saying, "But not for long." The inner picture of the cover innocent had been decorated with a red felt-tipped pen. It had a gash across its throat and blood ran down the front of its dress all the way to the ground.

Chapter 7

CRIGHTON was in the kitchen fixing supper, and Carson was on the phone calling Sterling Library at Yale. He asked for the duty officer and was astonished when the director himself came on.

"I am Rutherford Rogers, may I help you?" the librarian said.

"Great Scott!" Carson replied. "I apologize for bothering you. I thought all the officials would have gone home to supper, and I'd get the night staff. I'll try not to hold you any longer than I have to. My name is Steve Carson, and I'm a friend of Dr. Edward George."

"Yes, indeed. My distinguished predecessor."

"Right. Well, I'm trying to reach him, and no one answers at his home phone. I don't know if he's even in New Haven, and I was simply calling the library to see if anyone there knew what he's up to. I'm calling from Washington, by the way."

"No problem at all, Mr. Carson. And it's just as well you called, because there *is* no one at his home, so far as I know. He's on the West Coast. We had lunch together just before he left, and he told me he was going to spend a month at the Huntington Library, helping them computerize their rare book collection."

"Really? The last I heard he was convinced that the computer had destroyed librarianship as a profession."

Rogers laughed. "I think he still believes that, but he's been beaten down to the position that it's probably too late to stop, so he's dedicated himself to damage control. He's trying to keep the profession from putting anything in the computer that can still be done better by hand. He's still convinced the screen is a blindfold to the reader, not a window."

"That's the guy. Is he in good health?"

"For a seventy-year-old man, he's in better shape than I am. And of course, he's working harder than ever. I've never seen anyone who so enjoys living."

"I quite agree. Don't let me take any more of your time, and thank you so much, Dr. Rogers. With the three-hour differential, I may be able to catch him at work. Thank you for your courtesy and help."

"My pleasure. And tell him we miss him. We're very fond of him here. Get him back as quickly as possible."

Carson completed his goodbyes and shouted at Crighton, "Are you interruptible? I'm closing in on George."

"Be there in a minute."

Carson began his calls and he had both found the librarian emeritus and gotten through the salutations by the time Crighton came on the extension. "Hey!" she said, "It's so good to hear your voice!"

Talking on top of each other, they brought the older man up to date on their troubles, and Carson concluded, "So it's like old times, Dr. George. Confusion confounded. We need your advice, we need your dignified name, we need you! First, do you know any of the old Dumas Malone team so you could grill 'em for us?"

"Actually, I think John Ballard may still be with them, and he once worked for me at Yale. I'd be happy to ask him whatever questions you could use. What's your plan of action, Steve? Where do you go from here?"

"Well, here are the assumptions I'm working on, not necessarily in any order. Given: we need to find Steele. Given: wherever she was going apparently was within a half-day of Washington. If she had expected to be gone overnight, surely she'd have told Crighton. Question: what could she have hoped to find in a half-day's drive out of D.C. that would relate to those copies? Surely either where the collection once was or, more likely, where the collection is right now. Question: where could it be? Possibilities: in the original barn. In the neighboring house. In a big house not too far away—presumably it would have taken at least five or six wagonloads to move it secretly. But it had to be kept secret for a while, and God knows they must have been successful. No one's heard of it in a hundred and fifty years. That suggests it's never left the hands of the people who wanted it gone so Jefferson could get the money. Ergo cumquat sum: The collection was moved a short distance into a great house occupied by a family politically sympathetic to Jefferson, who have kept it intact to today. I'm simply going to figure out where it is and go there and ask if they've seen a good-looking college girl sometime in the past two days."

"Splendid!" said George.

"You're out of your mind," Crighton said.

"What possible flaw do you find?" Carson asked.

"Why you nut, you convinced me yourself. How much was a congressman paid in 1814?"

"What's that got to do with it?"

"Answer me," Crighton pursued.

"Well, probably eight or nine hundred a year or so."

"Okay. So Congress voted T. Jefferson twenty-four thousand dollars—twenty-five years' salary!—for those

53

"unneeded replacement" books. That's big money. The scandal that the loyal opposition could make with that kind of chicanery would have brought Jackson, or whoever was next, into the White House twenty years sooner. I'm telling you, whoever pulled this hide-some-and-buy-others stunt would have burned those books the next night and eaten the ashes."

"Not necessarily," Carson said firmly. "You can reason either backwards or forwards on this. You were probably speaking figuratively, but burning is about all you could do with those books. You couldn't throw 'em in the river, they'd float into someone's sight. You couldn't feed 'em to the cows, and you couldn't give 'em away without somebody noticing and the word getting out. And have you ever tried to burn a book? Almost impossible, even now when they're made of paper. In those days, they were one hundred percent rag. Working fast, you'd simply get a colossal mound of charred stench—but that's not really the point. The point is that people just don't destroy books. You might give 'em away or you might sell 'em, but you don't burn them or bury them. If somebody gave you three thousand books and said, 'Get rid of these, they're stolen,' you wouldn't destroy them, you'd cover 'em over with something while you decided what to do with 'em. Nobody could or would burn that library. But reasoning backward, I'm convinced nobody did, and that's what Steele found. The actual books themselves, not just the story about them, is what's going to make her rich. What do you think, Dr. George?"

"What I think is, I'm jealous of the fun you two are having. Yes, I think there's just enough to your theories that they're worth pursuing. And, Crighton, bad as they are, given the pressure you're under to find that woman, they're the best thing you've got for the moment. Your other avenue is the authorities, but they'll have to treat it as a missing-person problem, and that requires a seventy-two-hour wait before they're even permitted to start. No, weak as it is in spots, it is surely worth pursuing until you find out why it is *not* viable."

"Bless you, sir," said Carson, "I don't suppose there's a prayer that you could join us, is there?"

George laughed. "Well, I've done about all I can accomplish out here for the moment. Like any good consultant, the main thing I've achieved is to give the staff someone they can blame if what they wanted to do all along goes wrong. We've finished the planning stage, and they're about to start inputting the programs. I'd probably not be missed for a few days. Hmmm." He paused and then said, "I surely would love to be in on this with you two. Are you serious about my joining you?"

Crighton and Carson burst into a stream of supplications, and George said, "That's enough! I only needed the slightest reassurance. What time is it now? Four o'clock? I'll catch the red-eye flight and I should be in Dulles by sunup."

"Marvelous!" Carson shouted. "We'll come out and collect you."

"No, no. I'll just take a cab into the Minerva Club and I'll meet you there for breakfast. Eight o'clock."

"Won't you be exhausted?" Crighton asked with concern.

"Nonsense. The older I get the less sleep I need, and I sleep like a log on night airplanes. Day airplanes I stay awake on to help the pilot drive, but at night, he's on his own. I'll be fully refreshed by the time I see you. And the chance of reconvening the team is too good to miss. I'll see you in the Minerva lobby in time for grapefruit—and gas up a car. We should have those books in sight by tomorrow night."

They said their goodbyes and Crighton came out of the bedroom. Her relief was all too evident, but she said, "He's crazier than you are. How did I ever get mixed up with two such . . . come on. The food should be ready."

Chapter 8

F RIDAY morning. Steve, Crighton, and Edward George were sitting at a linen-draped table in the Minerva Club. The wide, curved window of the Garden Room was flooding the place with light, and the three were absorbing hurried mouthfuls of French toast and coffee. George was giving them a more detailed explanation of what he was doing on the Coast when he interrupted himself. "How soon can we get into the library?" he asked.

"Nine," Crighton said.

"Good. That gives us a few minutes to plan our attack. I think—"

"Hold it," Crighton broke in. "Before we get any deeper in this, I want to know about Alexa Lehman. Have you seen her? Are you keeping in touch?"

"I have, and she's just as charming and as interesting as ever," George said. "We met in the Weald in April, and stayed in Tunbridge Wells for a week. 'Oh to be in England, now that . . .' Just like Browning promised. Then she claimed I had to see Austria in the spring, so we had a second week in Innsbruck watching the snow melt. It

56

worked out remarkably well. The skiers were gone, and the tourists hadn't arrived, and the waterfalls just leaped into the valley like a travel poster. She does make life more attractive."

"Did she stay in Europe?" Crighton asked.

"For a month or so, and I came back to New Haven. Apparently she was in Washington up till a few weeks ago. Now she's back in Vienna for some kind of family business."

"Business," said Steve. "She seems wonderfully well heeled. Is that old family money, do you suppose? Serfs and castles and such?"

George laughed. "It may have been once, but that was all wiped out at the turn of the century, I gather. No, Alexa is very much a self-made woman. She was widowed during World War II—her husband had been a professor at the University of Dresden, and she was in Poland when the eastern front collapsed. The Russians overran all the civilians, and she was left on the wrong side of the line at the end of the war. It took her two years just to get back to what was left of Dresden. She spent the fifties working her way west via Austria, Switzerland, and England."

"Is she Polish, then?"

"No. Austrian. Viennese."

"Then where'd the money come from?"

"She worked for the Russians as a translator during the occupation, then she became a go-between between the German provincial governments and the communists. From there she got into the international banking scene, and she first came to America to report on the World Bank for three investment houses in Munich. She did the same thing for a number of Swiss banks until the seventies, when she retired. The money came from what she saw watching the money world. She simply parlayed her salary into a steadily growing surplus. Marvelous woman. Her mind is perpetually in gear."

"I'll never forget the first time we met her," Crighton said. "Some guy had made the mistake of asking her how she wanted to be addressed, and after she'd clarified that, she said, 'And I expect you to rise when I come into the room, open doors, and seat me at tables, but the moment our minds meet, I will resent it bitterly if you imply in any way that I am a woman.' Hah! I thought Carson's jaw was going to drop off right between his legs."

Steve grinned, "I don't deny it. Great woman. Has she still got that splendid apartment here in Washington? God! For a few brief moments I was being treated like the Lord so manifestly intended."

"She does, and speaking of your treatment, how are you being dealt with *these* days? This Williamsburg thing sounds like a great opportunity. Are you pleased with the way it's going?"

"Very much so. It could scarcely be better. We're digging the Davenport Hundred, you know. It was a stockaded farm across the river from Jamestown, and it's fascinating. The site itself is great sport, but watching the Williamsburgers work it is even greater. They've been at it so long and they're so professional, it's a joy just to eyedrop. When I did the Canyon de Chelley dig, most of the team was as new as I was, and we went at it like cold snails for fear of doing something irreparable. My Virginia friends simply roar along in comparison. It's the photograph, survey, measure, grid, strip, sieve, bottle, strip, sieve, photograph—everybody laughing and scratching and never missing a grain. Marvelous experience."

"I've always wondered about that perpetual measuring you archeologists do. Is it really necessary, or do you just do it to make it look hard? Awe the peasants."

"Blasphemy!" Steve laughed. "It is the very heart of the exercise! Sometime when we're stuck in traffic, I will give you an exhaustive lecture on the need for total measurement—up, down, across, and triangulated to the nearest benchmark."

"Save that till I'm along," Crighton said, "I've always been suspicious of all that measuring, too, but I didn't want to hurt your feelings."

"Oh? That's never stopped you before. Do you mean to tell me there are even more ways of keeping me down than the ones you've lashed me with already?"

"You've got it, Superman."

"No, you two Philistines," Steve said, "the measurement bit really got started in the Early Man department. For a century the great names would find a site and carefully search it—sieving and labeling and doing a reasonably good job on vertical sequence—working off two assumptions: One, that the site was occupied by a single family and you could learn how that family lived from what you found in that one place, and two, that what you found from the top down gave you an understanding of recent to earlier. Youngest to oldest. The time sequence has held up fairly well (though recording pollen and tree rings and carbon 13 do it with more precision), but those ideas about 'who used the site' have been shot to hell. Since most of the early man types were hunters and gatherers, it was believed that the male went out and hunted and gathered and brought it back to the reproducing female so she could feed herself and the offspring. Now everybody believes that a true hunter et cetera moved every few days or weeks and used different sites to do different things: fished by the creek, killed (or scavenged) by the water hole, cached carcasses up at the cave, and so on. And he took the whole family with him. So to get any idea of how any single family lived—even what they ate—you have to tie all the sites together into a family loop. And to tie different units together you have to know what pollen levels match which ones miles away,

59

which flint flakes reveal which maker at the stream site, the cache site, the hunting sites, and so on. In a nutshell—"

"Too late," Crighton said.

"In a nutshell, the trade has simply moved those prehistory archeological techniques over to modern-history archeology. By measurement we can tell which artifacts fell when the house was burned, which came from a buried body, which were dropped during the planting season, which matched the harvest, which were pre-European Indians and which stockade Indians. Et cetera. Or at least we try to. Recall, the whole idea of the game is to reconstruct three things: "What was it like?", "Why did it happen?", "What does it mean?"

"Are you getting close to the answers?" George asked.

"Don't ask. No, dammit. Every generation jerks everything the previous one said out of the wall and turns it inside out. I'm beginning to think there's no profession on earth that cannibalizes itself like archeology. Have you read any of the books recently?"

"Not for a generation. I was fascinated with the Egyptians and the Babylonians once."

"Well, you're the whole Olduvai Gorge story behind, but you didn't miss much. Everything the Leakeys proved has been unproved. There's a large group who believe that you can't tell what early man ate by looking at the bones in Leakey's sites for the simple reason that man's bones were there because whoever made the piles was eating *him*! This bunch think early man was a scavenger like the jackals and went around looking for the carnivores' refuse and rather frequently got eaten on the site. Would you believe that now we're not even sure that the agriculturists came *after* the hunters and the gatherers?"

"There," Crighton said, "aren't you sorry you asked?"

George laughed. "I think I'm looking for that traffic

jam so you can go through all that a bit more slowly. You lost me on the Leakeys."

"While I loved the lecture—" Crighton began.

"You're right, you're right. We've got to get down to business," George said. "Beloved troops, it's a delight to be here. You both look wonderful, and I feel like I'm back where I belong." He took a quick gulp of the last of his coffee and laid the napkin beside the plate. "We attack! Where do we stand? Have you alerted the police about the missing lady?"

"I have," Crighton replied. "I talked to Lieutenant Conrad and he agreed we'd done all we could under the circumstances. He said he'd load the data into the system so it would come on stream as soon as it was legal, but he'd do nothing till he'd talked to us. He said it sounded to him like a cat fight between two overeducated broads and we shouldn't get too up-tight over it."

Steve flinched. "Did you let him have it?"

"As when I'm dealing with you, I simply considered the source," Crighton said. "He'll never know how close he came. Have you got a plan, Dr. George?"

"Yes, a few thoughts have crossed my mind. Let's see how they match reality now that I'm here." George reached for a leather-bound note pad from a side pocket and laid it beside him on the table. "I agree with your thought that we've got to retrace your lady's steps, or at least her thinking—but it will have to be done like a skipping stone. We can only assume that the circling roommate must be getting closer, faster than we are, and that time is critical. I think there are several ways of breaking the puzzle, so we must simply pick the two that appear to have the best chances and divide them between Steve and me. I assume you need to make a living, Crighton."

"No, make that three best ways and let me have one. So long as no major crisis breaks loose at the library, I can work in-house—and anyway, I can steer you two around the place and save a little time. What choices are we picking from? Where do we start?"

"Very well," George said. "I agree with you that we should assume not only that the original books—the three thousand 1812 volumes—still exist but that the Steele woman has located them. Therefore, if we could figure out how *she* figured out where they were, we should either find her or find somebody who knows where she is. Our question then is: where are those books? Tell me again what the record said."

Steve lifted a spiral notebook from the floor beside him. "The report says, 'He then sent off three messengers into the country, one of whom obtained from Mr. John Wilson, whose residence is six miles from the city, the use of a cart and four oxen; it did not arrive at the office, until after dark on Monday night, when it was immediately laden with the most valuable records and papers, which were taken, on the same night, nine miles, to a safe and secret place in the country. We continued to remove as many of the most valuable books and papers, having removed the manuscript records, as we were able to do with our one cart, until the morning of the day of the battle of Bladensburg.'"

"Hmmm. That could suggest he saved the papers, but lost the library."

"No, he says flatly in his next-to-last paragraph, 'a number of the printed books were consumed but they were all duplicates of those which have been preserved.' All this was in a letter dated September 15. In one dated December 17, the clerk admits some of the cash receipts had had it, but he says the books have 'suffered no injury.'"

"December. . . ?"

"Eighteen-fourteen."

"I thought this was the War of 1812?"

62

"It was, but all that happened in 1812 was a bunch of naval battles. The Americans burned Toronto in 1813 and the British burned Washington in 1814 in revenge. The Capitol went up in flames in August and everyone was trying to pin the blame on somebody. The quotes are from a mess of reports and investigations that followed right after the disaster."

"Why *did* they wait so long to get the books out of the city?"

"According to the bureaucrats—and I'm inclined to sympathize with them—there was nothing in the newspapers saying the British were so close. Remember, they marched overland from Baltimore—came up the Chesapeake—and the War Department in the executive branch grabbed all the local horses and wagons and moved their stuff out before they told State and Treasury there might be trouble. They never did tell the legislature or the judiciary and by the time Congress heard it in the streets, all the local transport was long gone."

"Umm," said George.

"Forgive my hurrying you two," Crighton said with a slight edge to her voice, "but where are you headed with this thought, Dr. George?"

"Well, we can think about the situation from both ends. From the front end: the professional enemy is coming overland from the east, with thousands of uniformed veterans of the Napoleonic wars dragging artillery behind them. You've got four oxen and a cart. What would you do with them and which direction would you go? This gives you some rather-likelies and some not-very—like heading straight east on the Baltimore road.

"From the present end: you've got a mess of books that you know about, that can be reached in half a day from Washington. What kind of building are they in and where is it located? Who owns it and who's operating it?"

"I like the present target," Crighton said. "The building has to be fairly big, private—not open to the public like a museum or school—and probably not bought and sold too many times. Maybe never."

"Too broad," Carson said. "I think we should work with the historical scene. Take it from the beginning. There would only have been a single bridge over the Potomac—two at the most, by then—and there would have been very few houses built yet of any size. Remember, Washington only became a town in 1800. I think we should try to reconstruct where the books went originally, and then follow them logically through the years."

"Great if you've got a decade to do it in. We've only got . . . hell, it may be too late already. Dr. George, do you think Magnolia has found her yet?"

"We have no way of knowing. She hasn't done it any place public or it'd be on the news, so we have to assume she's looking like we are."

"How is *she* doing it?" Crighton asked.

"Good question," George replied. "I'd think she's calling everybody who might know and trying to guess what Steele learned from her own notes."

"Damn," said Carson. "Good point. She has a lot of the facts from the front end, doesn't she? But no, I don't think that's what she's doing—she'd have gone through all that while she was steaming back at U. Va. I think she's parked somewhere waiting for Steele to come back. At Crighton's or the Library of Congress or at some guy's—girl's—house that she thinks she'll come home to. Remind us to see if anyone's sitting in a car when we go home next."

"Okay," Crighton said. "Let's get started. I assume you want us to split up, Dr. George? Not work together?"

"Yes. Until somebody hits pay dirt, then we can all join in and follow what they've found. Shall we use you as the crossing point, Crighton? Everybody calls Crighton every hour on the hour. All right?"

"Okay, except I won't be there for a bit. Give me two hours before you start checking in. I'm going to try the property bit first. Real estate. I'll be at the Werner-Bok by eleven o'clock."

Carson said, "I think I'll look for some expertise and then work the stacks to try some shortcuts. You heading out, Dr. George?"

"No, I'm going to start on the phone. I'll do it from my room here. I think your original idea to go straight to Dumas Malone's Jefferson team had great merit. Let's move. Time is wasting—and as soon as anyone finds anything that even seems warm, pass it around. It might give meaning to somebody else's leads."

They went their separate ways, purposefully, each lost in his or her own thoughts.

Chapter 9

S TEVE Carson was the first to get the quest in gear. George had disappeared into the Minerva Club's elevator and Crighton had gone out the front door. Carson rushed into a phone booth off the lobby, and a moment later he was talking to Wilford Gilbert, head of the history department at The College of William and Mary.

Salutations past, he said, "So I asked myself, 'Carson,' I said, calling myself by name, 'Carson, who knows more live historians than anyone else in America?' And I answered, 'W. Gilbert, the walking Cardex of W. and M.'"

"What the futz are you talking about? What do you want out of me?"

"I want to know who, in the environs of our nation's capital, knows anything about the War of 1812."

"Eighteen-twelve? Nobody gives a damn about . . . Who cares? That is not fashionable, Carson. That's like asking who's the leading biographer of Franklin Pierce."

"I know that, and I haven't time to explain my aberration, so just cut the editorial and give me a name. Is there a living soul inside the Capital Beltway that has the faintest familiarity with that lost episode in the nation's history?"

"Well, actually, there are two such aberrants, believe it or not. They're with the National Park Service up there. The Park Service got stuck with Fort McHenry in Baltimore—Star Spangled Banner place, you know—and a L'Enfant fort down on the Potomac. They hired a couple of historians to do the signs and folders and the two just stayed on. I can't remember either of their names—has something to do with drakes or ducks or something—but if you go over to the Park Service you ought to be able to flush 'em out. If we're to believe their journal articles, they hate each other's you-know-whats—they're always taking swipes at the other guy's last piece, but I don't know how they relate in the flesh."

"Love it! That's just what I need. If anything comes of any of this, I'll give you a full report when I see you. I should be back in Williamsburg this weekend. I'll buy you a beer. Two beers. Goodbye."

A phone call and a taxi got him in front of a remarkably drab government office building that was identified by an aluminum sign on the lawn as the headquarters of the National Park Service. Once inside, he was directed to a long, low room that looked like it ought to hold blank forms for the Veterans Administration but instead housed two dozen or so historians, each allocated a steel desk, a filing cabinet, and a three-shelf bookcase. The experts he sought turned out to be called Fowler and Jones. So much for ducks and drakes as a mnemonic hook, Carson thought.

"This doesn't look quite like how I thought the Park Service would be housed," Carson tried for the friendly opener. "I guess I thought you'd be in a peeled-bark lodge or something."

This brought no reply at all. The two historians were in their fifties, tweedy with sweaters, and they looked remarkably alike. Their desks sat on either side of an aisle, with a single chair between them. Carson sat down on the chair and slid it back slightly to improve his view, but he still found himself flipping his head back and forth like a judge at a tennis match.

"Right," he said. "Well, let's get straight to why I'm here. We are trying to trace where the records of the Congress were taken just before the British burned the Capitol. According to the written record, a couple of the library clerks put everything into an ox cart and in several trips got the goods to a 'safe place nine miles out of the city.' The question is, Where was this safe place? Was there anything inherent in the historical situation of the time that would give us any clues?"

Fowler opened his mouth to speak, but Jones beat him to it. "That should not be too difficult. When the British were first sighted coming up the Chesapeake Bay, our army and the local militia went straight east out of Washington and headed for Annapolis. Then when the British landed and started back toward the Capitol, the troops in the field sort of crumpled up and began to lose a series of engagements in a sort of rolling retreat. The officers recognized they were in trouble and began to send couriers back to the War Department urging evacuation. I believe they called this 'bugging out' in Vietnam. On receiving this recommendation, the government clerks started to load up their offices and move everything inland. It was all supposed to be very secret, but the word leaked out to wives and sweethearts, and suddenly all the civilians in Washington were putting their valuables in their vehicles and making a mad dash for the country."

"In what direction?" Carson asked.

"I was about to tell you. Everybody headed toward Virginia. They went straight up Pennsylvania Avenue to Rock Creek—which had a little two-lane bridge over it then—and then through Georgetown to the river. There were two huge traffic jams at the creek and at the Potomac. There was no Georgetown bridge then, so everybody ferried over to Roosevelt Island (which they knew as Mason's Island) and took a causeway off north and west toward Leesburg."

"How long did this go on?"

"Two days—right up to the time the British burned the White House."

"Was this flight just the citizens, or did the government go that way, too?"

"Everybody. They moved the State Department and the Treasury inland, and you remember that Dolley Madison stayed till the last minute to restrain the panic. At the last possible moment, she seized the Constitution and the Bill of Rights and rolled them up in a rug, and she took Gilbert Stuart's portrait of Washington off the wall. She threw everything in the back of a buggy—and got caught in the traffic jam at Rock Creek like everybody else."

"Was the president with the army?"

"No, he and one dragoon followed Dolley on horseback about an hour after she started. He spent all that night and the following day—which was a howling hurricane, by the way—trying to find her in Virginia. He finally came back east across the Potomac up near Point of Rocks and rejoined the army outside Baltimore. It was a remarkable feat for a sixty-year-old man in pouring rain."

"That has nothing whatsoever to do with the answer to this man's question," Fowler managed to cut in. "Except that since everybody else was going to Leesburg, anyone fleeing from the Capitol building would almost certainly have taken the Fourteenth Street Bridge to Alexandria."

"Was there a Fourteenth Street Bridge then?" Carson asked.

"It was the *only* bridge across the Potomac—two bridges, actually. There was a drawbridge at this end beside where Engraving and Printing now stands, then a long dirt causeway out to the river where a second drawbridge crossed the main channel. When the British set fire to the city, the Americans burned the first drawbridge to keep the enemy from following them to Virginia."

"The next night the British burned the other drawbridge to keep the Americans from coming back," Jones said loudly to show he knew as much about it as Fowler.

"But there were no traffic jams on the Long Bridge—that's what they called it then. *That's* the way an ox cart would have gone," Fowler said flatly. "You said the cart went out and back. The Leesburg route was so jammed there was no way anybody could go against the grain. You get lots of stories of people trying to get back into Washington to rescue their children and nobody could do it. They were pushed off the road and mashed at culverts and crossings. But the Long Bridge kept running both ways till they burned it."

"Then where did the roads go once they got on the Virginia side?" Carson asked.

Fowler turned to Jones, "If you'd give me Wilkinson back, I could show him."

"I returned it the same day I borrowed it. It's there under your bookcase."

Fowler frowned and got up to reclaim a large map rolled up and lying on the floor. He spread it on his desk toward Carson. "Wilkinson's map is 1816, so the time is right, and as you can see there were still only two ways to Virginia, no matter what. One was that one of his to Leesburg—up at the north through Georgetown, and the other went off the end of the Long Bridge south to Alexandria. Everything around where the Pentagon and National Airport are now was mud swamp. Reeds and tidal muck. The road off the Long Bridge actually lay on tidal creek banks all the way to Alexandria."

"And you think that's the way an ox cart would have

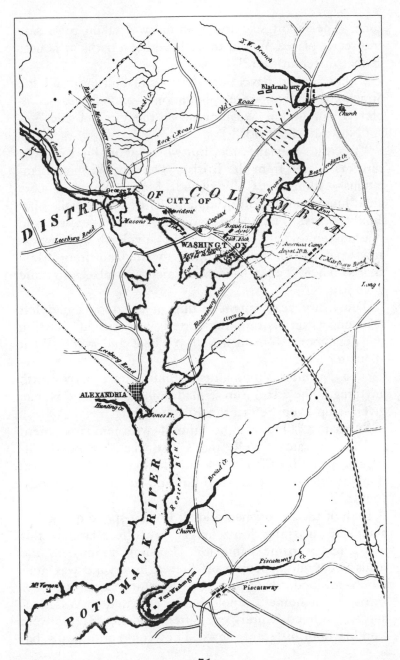

71

gone? The report said the material was taken to 'a safe and secret place.' Would there have been barns or houses in that direction then?"

"There would have been barns and houses in all the directions. There were plantations—and farms—completely surrounding Washington on the Virginia side."

"Not the Maryland?"

"Yes, the Maryland, too, but we are assuming that your cart was fleeing from the British. The local Virginia plantations—Arlington, Collingwood, Mount Vernon—were great huge things. The Maryland farms were small, one-family tracts. They sold produce to Georgetown and Washington. The Virginians were involved with wheat and wool, which they shipped to England from Alexandria. There would have been plenty of places to store your papers."

Too many years spent sitting in classrooms had left their impact on his thinking pattern, and without noticing the derailment, Carson asked, "Wheat and wool? What about tobacco?"

"No. Northern Virginia never could grow tobacco worth anything. They still can't. Bad soil. The planters had given it up even before the Revolution."

"Amazing." He caught himself with embarrassment and hastily said, "Well, that's just what I needed. Although you differ on *where* in Virginia, neither of you think they'd have gone to Maryland to hide the goods. Right?"

Both of the historians nodded. Fowler spoke quickly to anticipate anything Jones might say, "Remember, this was a real wartime panic rout. Pushing wagons off the roads and pulling people off horses. Everyone was genuinely terrified. *We* know how the story came out—the British went home, Napoleon was defeated at Waterloo, and we all lived happily ever after. But the 1812ers were working from different views. They could still hardly believe that the thirteen little colonies had gotten free from mighty England. England had lost colonies before and had always come back and retaken them—India, parts of Canada, Caribbean islands. In the back of everyone's mind was the thought that this was England returning. The enemy was so big and so powerful. Flight would have been to the interior. Run away! Because of the way the rivers lay, Maryland was a pocket leading nowhere. Virginia was open-ended."

"Gottcha. You've convinced me. In case I need some dates and places, who're the big names in this period?"

"Do you mean bibliographically? Where should you go for reading about the Madison period?"

"Exactly."

"I would suggest my own volumes," Jones said stiffly. "Otherwise, possibly Irving Brant."

"I have written extensively on the Federalists myself," Fowler said in a slight falsetto.

"Oh, yes. Of course. I was taking both of your own canons as a given. And I do thank you. I am much in your debt. I hope I can call you back if I get into trouble." Carson struggled to his feet and expressed his gratitude with conviction. He shook hands and headed out of the building.

The secret to this thing, he thought, is narrowing the possibles. Crighton was right. Those books and that woman could be anywhere and it could take months to find them—unless we can slice off the unlikelies. Where is it most unlikely that she could be? The first pass, he thought, had just gone reasonably well. He'd eliminated one state and two directions. Not bad. Back to the Werner-Bok.

73

Chapter 10

EDWARD George had gone directly to his room, removed his jacket, and drawn a chair up to the phone on the bedside table. Rejecting the telephone directory with an irritated "no" (based on endless frustrations with its labyrinthine front sections), he dialed information and started to work. Twenty minutes later he replaced the phone and began to write in his notebook. In this manner he used up another five minutes abstracting his past conversations plus an additional five listing all the questions that the conversations had stimulated beyond the ones they had answered. At the close of the exercise, he put the notebook into his jacket pocket, put the jacket on, and headed to the street.

The doorman asked, "May I get you a cab, sir?"

"I'd be grateful. I am going to the Werner-Bok Library."

The cab stair-stepped toward the Mall, creeping through student-laden streets on the George Washington University campus, working its way around sightseers in front of the White House, and finally accelerating alongside the Treasury building. George leaned forward, staring at each monument like a tourist on his first trip to the big city, although he had been here many times before.

What a marvelous, magnificent place it is, he thought. It really is incredible how well it has aged, and how well it holds together. It must be the Roman columns that do it. Even if you're building across a two-hundred-year period, the columns make it look like you did it all at the same time.

Archives, with even more columns than par came up on his right, and he was smiling at the excess when the cab pulled to a stop in front of the Werner-Bok Library sitting solidly on the Mall between the National Gallery and the Natural History Museum. He paid the driver and walked carefully around the dampened pavement where spray from the Meeting of the Waters fountain was blowing on the sidewalk.

Great stuff, he thought. Roman for government, Renaissance for art. You can't beat it.

He started up the cascade of steps to the main piazza and made a mental note that he must think about why they do work so well. Have we all been taught that fluted columns go with governing and acanthus leaves with culture, or did the architects know what kind of boxes to put them in so that the skin really does fit the contents. Metaphysically. Or something. Intriguing. Must work on that some time.

The huge bronze doors were already open and he went purposefully into the Great Hall, where he threaded his way among the display cases and slanted off toward the director's office. He'd been doing this two or three times a year for several decades now. I wonder how Brooks is holding up, he thought.

The secretary ushered him into the ornate office, where the director rose from behind an enormous carved desk and shouted, "Edward George! What a splendid surprise.

75

God, it's good to see you. Sit down, sit down. You're looking marvelous. My goodness, retirement is clearly agreeing with you."

"It is, and you look simply terrible yourself," George replied as he sank into the leather chair Brooks had pointed him to. "I was just standing outside this box thinking how well you've housed the collection, and then I see this office of yours and I'm always surprised all over again. I can never remember how splendidly your predecessors cased themselves. Look at this! Frescoes and plaster muses and paneling up to your earlobes. Your coffin won't be half as fine—and speaking of coffins, you look like you're more than halfway there. What in heaven's name is the matter with you?"

"Actually, it's nothing in particular. Fifteen years of dedicated leadership beginning to show."

"Burnout?"

"Possibly. Lost purpose might be a better way of putting it."

"I wish I didn't know what you meant, but I'm afraid I do. I've been seeing too much of it among our generation of librarianship. I'm beginning to think it's the sense of guarding treasures of the mind that we can't quite remember what good they are to anyone anymore. We've kept stored knowledge like holy relics and fewer people believe in relics all the time. I once had the pleasure of breaking bread with Mortimer Adler—you know, the Hundred Great Books Britannica man—and I must admit I went into it thinking he had badly oversimplified everything, but I came out considerably shaken. Dan Boorstin had asked him what he thought the Library of Congress should save, and he replied that the secret was to burn everything older than fifty years and keep burning as time went on. So long as you kept the last fifty year's worth of nonfiction—he excluded belles-lettres—he claimed you'd always have what you needed. Why? Because every profession carries along what matters in its new books and junks the myths and the mistakes of the earlier generations. Jacques Barzun used to say that every book was like a sandwich—the first half was old stuff getting the reader ready to understand the new stuff that was coming; the last half was obvious stuff explaining the little slice of meat that was actually new in the middle, and the middle was really all you wrote the book for. Adler says the first piece of bread is always brought along, so you don't need the old books and even if you have 'em, no one looks at them."

"Ummm," Brooks replied. "You do know what I'm talking about. 'No one looks at them.' That gets right to the heart of the problem. The reading rooms aren't used a third as much as when I came into librarianship. I did a tour of national libraries in Europe last year after IFLA, and I was appalled at the empty rooms I looked at. Unless a library is tied to a teaching program where the students have to parrot something back, there's dust on every table over there, and on too many of ours here. Where have we failed?"

"You know as well as I do, it's not a failure in librarianship, it's simply a change in the way we do research. You don't build a total bibliography to get a Ph.D. anymore, you pick a minute topic on the fringe of the subject and do current research about it. Retrospective research is gone everywhere. The young people say, what difference does it make what they thought about women's rights or prison reform or railroad regulation fifty years ago? What matters is right now with the problem pummeled with today's variations. Unfortunately, I can't think why they're wrong—except it plays hell with our circulation statistics."

"Precisely. And what is sucking me dry, Ed," Brooks ran a hand through what the magazines always referred to as his "distinguished mane of white hair," "is that I can't decide whether to tread water here for another five years till I can retire, or take a twenty-thousand-dollar cut to go back and run some ivy-covered college library somewhere."

"I sympathize with you, but just to make the choice even harder, let me remind you that that little ivy-covered library you picture so clearly is either so desperately short of cash that you would spend half your time trying to raise money from people who think libraries are as purposeless as you must if you leave here, or, small and ivy-covered though it may be, is full of microfilmed serials, computerized catalogs, unionized desk attendants, deteriorating volumes, and overcrowded stacks. Camelot has a second mortgage for us, too."

"Then, goddammit, why do you look so cheerful?"

"Because I'm taking it a day a time and playing by my own rules—and leaving poor sons-of-bitches like you to carry the responsibility of institutions you're too honest to put down. Being age seventy is one of the few excuses for hedonism that is still accepted. And that reminds me of why I'm here bothering you. I want a stack pass."

"Our pleasure. What's the project?" Brooks asked.

"You'd never know it from the way I've been running off at the mouth, but I haven't got time to tell you. But if you'd point me to your books on Thomas Jefferson, I promise to give you a complete report when we come out the other side. With your permission, I'd like to use Crighton Jones's office downstairs as a place to hang my hat."

"I'll have Mrs. Ferrar give you the proper papers—and speaking of Crighton, we must talk about her. I don't think she'll be with us much longer."

"What? Career development or fired?"

"Both. We'll talk about it."

George moved on to the outer office where the ever-efficient Mrs. Ferrar quickly provided the necessary forms. He thanked her warmly, and sped out the door.

Now frowning intently, he moved through the marble halls, headed for the working heart of the library.

When at last on station, he slowed to the deliberate rhythm of the ancient ritual of research: obeisance at the catalog, irrationally long wait at an elevator, the plunge into aromatic stacks, and finally the quick and hopeful scan to find the stored knowledge—in this case that of the Federalist period neatly organized and shelved before him like a spectrum of thought and memory. Cursing quietly over the fact that the goddamned bifocals only worked for book spines from his chin's height down, he set to work.

Chapter 11

WHEN Crighton had left the Minerva Club, she had thanked the doorman for his proffered taxi, but said she was walking and proceeded to do so at a fast clip down Massachusetts Avenue toward Dupont Circle. Her first stop was at the drugstore across from the Metro stop where she bought a "Tourist's Map to Your Nation's Capital." She opened it across the Washington Monument thermometers and the White House paperweights and reassured herself that it covered what she wanted, refolded and paid for it, and hurried out the door to come to an abrupt stop at the curb.

Before her was a whirling stream of apparently unending traffic, spinning around the three concentric circles, nine lanes wide and as remorseless as the Amazon. As she watched the unending flow, she recalled having read somewhere that there actually were 135 traffic lights in this particular street pattern and she thought, Why don't any of them stop the damn cars? Much too late for her preferred tempo, they did manage to interrupt the tide long enough for pedestrians to sprint into the central park

itself, and she hurried past the Admiral's fountain to re-
peat the wait and sprint out the other side. One more
block down Massachusetts and she hurried up the steps of
a well-kept building that looked like it should be on a
Parisian boulevard. The bronze plaque to the right said it
was the original home of Andrew Mellon, secretary of the
treasury and father of the National Gallery of Art. A newer
plaque to the left identified the building as the current
home of the National Trust for Historic Preservation.
Crighton rushed up the steps and through a mosaicked
lobby—to come to a full stop before a wide desk with a
matron to match blocking all further passage.

"Yes?" the woman said. It was a personal challenge.

"Hi. Could I go into your library for a moment,
please?"

"Are you a member of the Trust?"

"Well, as a matter of fact I am." This unlikely distinc-
tion had resulted from a spring garden tour a couple of
years back when she had been asked to take tickets at the
door of Decatur House. She let the history lie and said,
"But I've had business dealings with the librarian on occasion."

"Which one?"

"I'm sorry. I've forgotten her name. Do you have more
than one?"

"We have three."

"Well, could I go see them?"

"I'll call them. What's your name?"

Crighton extracted her plastic pass from the Werner-
Bok Library and shoved it toward the woman. The matron
appeared surprised at the official linkage, and Crighton
wondered who—or what—the woman had thought she
was.

"Where is the library? I'll start ahead while you're calling."

The guardian motioned to a staircase behind her, and

Crighton charged down. The library filled the whole base-ment, low-ceilinged and crowded with tables, desks, and book stacks. A stylish young woman of her own age was hanging up the phone as she came through the door.

"Crighton Jones? Hello! We've talked so often I feel I should know you. I'm Susan Hobbs. How can I help?"

Crighton laid her purse and the map on a study table and said, "I was beginning to despair of ever getting in here. Why the third degree at the door? Have you had some kind of trouble or something?"

Hobbs sighed. "That woman! Her sole responsibility is to direct visitors to the proper people in the place, but apparently the only way she can get life satisfaction is to act like she *is* the trust. It's very frustrating. She's been talked to a dozen times."

"I suppose you do have to sort out the tourists from the members."

"No, no. We're happy to help anyone who's working with old buildings. We have folks who are rehabilitating their own places and architects redoing monuments and city managers setting up historic districts. That's what we're here for. If we've got something that can do any-body any good we're wide open. What can we do to help you?"

"Without wasting your time with all the background, I'm trying to find out what houses that were standing in 1814 are still standing today. Wait a minute! Not every-where. Just in a strip around Washington. Gimme a sec-ond."

She hurriedly opened her map of the Washington area and spread it on a table. She then tore off a strip of paper from the bottom edge, which she folded to give it body and then laid across the scale line under the legend at the top. Using a ball point pen, she made a mark at one end of her paper, measured off five miles and fifteen miles from this point, and then laid the mark on top of the Capitol building on the map. She grubbed around in her purse until she found a safety pin with which she skewered the strip to the Capitol. She then stuck the ball point through the five-mile point and started to draw.

"Wait a minute. Let me help," Hobbs said. "I'll hold the pivot. You draw."

Between them they quickly had two circles looping across the map.

"Thank you," Crighton said. "As you can see, we've now got a strip from five miles up to fifteen miles all the way around the Capitol building. If I wanted to find out what's still standing in that strip that was there in 1814, have I got a snowball's chance in hell? Has the Trust for Preservation done a census of historic houses or its moral equivalent?"

Hobbs grinned. "No, we haven't. We know everything there is to know about the houses that we preserve ourselves, but other people have to do all the work and then convince us we should assume responsibility for what they're trying to get us to take over. But there is a way you can do it. Do you know about HABS? The Historic American Buildings Survey?"

"I've heard of it vaguely."

"Well, back in the Depression, one of the WPA-kind of things was set up to help unemployed teachers and architects, and they set out to do what they called measured drawings of every building in America that was older than the Civil War or something. Believe it or not, they almost brought it off! There are tens of thousands of the drawings. They were all sent to the Library of Congress back in the thirties, and then when everybody got interested in preservation in the sixties the National Park Service got in the act, and now everybody is contributing to it. So far as your problem is concerned, though, all you'd have to do is get the HABS register and look at it by county. It's organized by state and then by county or city, and within each one of these, every old building is described, there's a description of precisely where it is, when it was built, who's lived in it, what condition it's in, and a drawing of all the important parts. It'll show you the four facades and the floor plans, and if it has any unusual details—like fireplaces and staircases and stuff like that—they'll be drawn too. The HABS sheets are fascinating. You go to look for one thing and an hour later you're still browsing!"

"My God, I think you've saved us. Wait a minute, though. Where are these things? And can ordinary people look at them?"

"Oh, sure. We have hundreds here for things we've been interested in, but the Library of Congress has the originals and anybody can use them. You can copy them there, too. But not too long ago a private company put the whole set on microfiche, and now any historical society or university library will have a set."

"You don't happen to know if the Werner-Bok has one, do you?"

"I don't know, but I'd be surprised if they didn't. Would you like to look at some here?"

"Maybe just long enough to see what they are. How much trouble would it be?"

"No problem. I'll be right back."

She returned promptly carrying an ordinary file folder full of an inch or so of sheets.

"Here's Arlington County. You can see what they look like."

Crighton opened the folder in front of her and found that what had appeared to be loose sheets were actually packets of two and three pages each stapled together. The first page carried a picture of the front of the building about the size of a playing card, with text describing the who, when, and where. The remaining page or two in each set were floor plans and elevations.

"That's enough. I've got the drift—and it is exactly

what I need. I'm off now, but I may be back. Keep your fingers crossed. If the Werner-B has its own set, we are in like Flynn. Bless you thrice over. I'll call you in a few days and tell you how this all came out, if I'm not back in person."

She said her goodbyes and ran up the stairs, stopping long enough to pick up her ID card from the matron's desk. Before the guardian could speak, Crighton gave her an icy look and headed for the door.

"Goddammed service people who hate to give service. May they fry in hell."

Chapter 12

At fifteen minutes before eleven, George entered Crighton's office to find Steve Carson holding a telephone to his ear. Carson held the pose without speaking for a few more moments and returned the receiver to its cradle.

"Hail, sire!" he said. "Have a seat. I was just trying Crighton's apartment to see if Sister Steele might be there. No answer. Either it's empty or blown away."

George sat down very deliberately and asked, "Is Crighton back yet?"

"No sign. She said to give her till eleven, and she's still got a few minutes. How has your morning gone?"

"Remarkably well. I actually found most of what I was after. And yours?"

"I could hardly believe it. Everything went like clockwork. I'm eager to report."

"Well, don't. Hold on till Crighton gets here and then we can bring everybody up to date at once. Where do we stand timewise? How long has it actually been now since Crighton last saw that woman?"

Carson seized the bridge of his nose and closed his

eyes. "Let's see. Crighton brought her home with her Tuesday night. They parted after breakfast on Wednesday morning. She didn't show up Wednesday night, and Crighton got that phone call the same evening. Crighton called me Thursday morning—yesterday. I came up and we called you last night. It's now nearly eleven o'clock on Friday. That makes it—let's say the woman must have been okay at least as of the threatening phone call—Wednesday night to Thursday night to now. Thirty-six hours. What's your guess? Has the nemesis closed in yet?"

"Obviously it's hard to know," George replied, "but I'm afraid it does not look good. Surely Crighton would have heard something by now if the woman—what is her name? Steele?—were delayed for any rational reason. Any time during the day she could have left word here at the library. Evenings Crighton has been home. No, not good. But we've got to act as if she can be found and warned even if I'm not sanguine myself."

"Sanguine. As in optimistic, or bloody? No, I think I'm a little more hopeful than you are. I keep thinking that the Steele woman set out to lean on somebody and brought it off. She made some kind of a haul—cash or rare books or some kind of triumph—and hung a party or drugs or booze on it and she's going to turn up sheepish but successful. What I'm afraid of is she'll walk back on the scene all wide-eyed, and Magnolia will knock her off before our open arms. No. Time is still with us, but of the essence. Hey! Comes the lovely Jones."

Crighton rushed in with a wave and pitched purse and map on her desk.

"You beat me," she said breathlessly. "How long have you been here?"

"Long enough to establish that your Steele woman is not answering the phone in your apartment—or if the Magnolia is sitting there instead, she isn't taking calls."

Crighton shuddered and George said, "You're right on

87

schedule. Time is wasting. Let's see where we stand. Problem: assuming that the Steele woman is or was where the lost library is or was, where is that? Who's first?"

"Me," said Crighton.

She scooped up the map from her desk and opened it on top of Steve's books spread across the work table.

"This circle," she said, "is five miles out from the Capitol building—the paper said the ox cart went nine miles to a safe place—and this other circle is fifteen miles. That gives us a little leeway in case they had to take the long way round or their measuring was sloppy. I think we should start looking inside this strip."

"Once again, what makes you think the books haven't been moved since they were first stored?" George asked.

"Steve believes that anything that out of the ordinary would have been picked up by history, and God help me, I'm beginning to agree with him. It's just barely possible that in the confusion of the war and the burning, the books might have been moved out of town with nobody but a few 'in' types really knowing where they went, but after that, no. He thinks moving three thousand books across the country would almost certainly have gotten somebody's attention, and I suspect he's right. If the fool things exist at all—and I'm still not as sure of that as you two seem to be—they're probably either right where they were first put or awfully close to it."

"Well said," Carson declared, "and let the record show, I'm now more convinced than ever that they do exist."

"Strangely enough, my last hour nearly converted me, too," George said. "More of that later. But for the immediate moment, do we have the faintest idea where in this circle of yours the place might be?"

"I can tell you where it probably isn't," Carson said. "According to two experts at the National Park Service, an ox cart full of good books would have gone right down that street there to the Fourteenth Street Bridge precisely where it is now, turned left off the end and headed south toward Alexandria.

Not east because that's where the British were, not north because that's where they were afraid the British soon would be, not west because the ferry in that direction was clogged with civilians. Just down in that quadrant right there." He swept his fingers from the Potomac toward the southwest.

"But wait a minute," Crighton said. "You're saying Virginia. The Triple-A map on her bed was for Maryland."

There was momentary silence all around and then Carson said, "Hold it. Can you remember, had the map been opened, or was it new?"

"No, as I remember it it was brand new. It was still tightly folded and no one can get a map back exactly the way it started."

"Then how does this sound? Steele sails into the Charlottesville Triple-A office and says give me a Washington map. Clerk hands over her usual kit of three. One is for the center of town—a tourist map, the monuments and downtown streets. One is for Maryland and the other for Virginia since the town laps over into both. Steele grabs all three and goes. Steele gets here, uses the city map to find the Library of Congress and the Werner-Bok, and leaves the other two in her briefcase. Wednesday, before she starts out, she looks for the one she needs for the day, grabs it, and goes out the door. She takes the Virginia one with her and leaves Maryland behind since she's not going to Maryland. The fact that you found a Maryland map on her bed proves she's in Virginia!"

George laughed and said, "That's about as logical as anything else we've heard here, but your park historians are a bit more convincing. I think we should go with the Virginia target."

"Then with a little bit of luck, I can get closer than that," Crighton said. She strode to her phone and dialed as she talked. "There's a directory of old houses that will tell us which ones are standing now that would have been standing then. Hello? This is Crighton Jones down in the

Press Office. Do we have something called HABS? It's supposed to be a huge microfiche collection. We do? Right here in the library? We'll be right up."

Forty-five minutes later the three were headed down the George Washington Memorial Parkway holding six paper-clipped packets of sheets from the friendly in-house copy machine. Carson was saying, "No, I agree with you. If those books are anywhere at all, the odds are at least fifty-fifty that Steele is at one of those six places."

"What was the final mix?" George asked.

"Well, we had twenty-one buildings that were 1814 or older. Eight or ten were open to the public, so the books couldn't be *there*. Everybody would know."

"Did you finally decide that Mount Vernon was within the nine-mile strip?"

"Oh, yes. There was no doubt that Mount Vernon—and Collingwood and Woodlawn—were right at nine or ten miles. The problem was Pohick Church and George Mason's Gunston Hall. They fell right on the outer edge if you measure as the crow flies, but since the roads then would have had to stay back of the creek heads, they'd surely be too far."

Crighton said, "That left about ten possibles that are still privately owned—in fact, most of the ten are in the hands of the original families yet. Two of these were already half-ruined when they were surveyed, so even if they've been restored, anything within the walls would have been shot. And two were just too small to hold three thousand books. That left these six." She waved the sheets.

"Ummm," George said. "Three thousand books at a pound each is a ton and a half. Following your thinking, we're probably looking for the best cellar."

They had now driven past National Airport and through Alexandria and were a mile down the Parkway with the Potomac on their left. Carson was at the wheel with Crighton beside him. George leaned over from the rear seat to look at the papers.

90

"So what's your search plan? How are we proceeding?"

"I thought we'd work Crighton's crescent starting from the river and going on around to the west," Carson replied. "Anyway, I think the house on the river is the best bet of the bunch, no matter where we start."

Crighton handed the top packet back. "He's probably right. It's Belvoir—the Lord Fairfax house. It's the largest of the mess, and it's got more outbuildings than any except the Glebe. We'll hit the Glebe last. It's the farthest around the strip."

"How could the Fairfax house still be in private hands? He was Washington's friend, wasn't he—and the wife was supposed to have been George's true love?" George asked.

"That's the one," Carson replied, "but according to the sheets, the original Fairfaxes took off for England just before the Revolution—thus neatly missing numerous years of Chaos and Old Night, no doubt—and another family took over the abandoned property in 1775. And kin of the second family have been there ever since."

"That's true of the Glebe, too," Crighton said. "When they disestablished the Anglican Church during the Revolution, the vicar stayed on in the manse, and the family name has been in the house all along. Of course that's true of most of these buildings. From our point of view, this one-family bit not only makes it easier to hide things without outsiders knowing, but also makes a little judicious blackmail more likely, if that's what Durance was up to."

"Did she seem capable of that sort of thing?" George asked.

"Oh, yes. She was so mad at somebody, I'm ready to believe she's capable of anything. Not only capable but effective at it, too."

"Nine miles. Mount Vernon coming up on the left," Carson said.

"A bunch of our rejected buildings turn up along here," Crighton remarked. "There's a 1770 mill up ahead on the right, and one of the too-small private homes is just down the road behind it. Woodlawn's up ahead. Wait a minute. There's a sign for Belvoir!"

An archetypical historic sign pointed to the left. BELVOIR MANSION. SEAT OF THE FAIRFAX FAMILY. BUILT 1741. OPEN 9:00-4:30.

"Damn," Carson said. "I thought this was supposed to be in private hands. Scratch Belvoir. On to the next one. What's number two?"

"Well, the sheet says Belvoir's private," Crighton said defensively. "Oops. The sheet's dated 1935. Should have thought of that. Not good. The next one is Green Spring Farm. Built in 1795. Big, rambling stone house with stone outbuildings. Wait a minute. We can get there faster by doubling back and cutting over to U.S. 1."

"I'll run into Belvoir and make a U in their parking lot."

Carson turned left across the Parkway and started down an asphalt road that had been covered with gravel to sustain the colonial ambience. The road proceeded directly toward the Potomac with huge and ancient trees overhanging it from either side, and just as Carson was beginning to think he was trapped in a much longer cul-de-sac than he had intended, the road came out onto a typical great-house-and-colonial-park scene. Carson made a quick left into a nearly empty car park and circled across empty parking spaces to head back out the way they had come.

"Wait! Wait! There it is!" Crighton shrieked. "Her car! There. The red Porsche! Get closer!"

Carson angled across more empty spaces to the gleaming sports car that had caught Crighton's attention. It sat alone, no other car for several rows toward the mansion.

"Look. A University of Virginia parking sticker. We've done it! We've found her."

"Jesus H. Christ," said Carson. "I will be damned."

George beamed and said, "Splendid, family, just splendid. You have indeed done it. But gently, folks. We have found her car. The question is, Have we also found the lady?"

Chapter 13

CARSON pulled alongside the Porsche and killed the engine.

"Let's be sure she isn't in it," he said as he slid out the door. He peered through the windows, tried each door, and beat on the trunk lid. After listening intently at the cracks, he straightened up and said, "Everything locked tight, and nobody seems to be home."

"So what do we do now?" Crighton asked.

"Good question," George replied. "I think our next move is quite important. We must not go in half-cocked."

Carson looked quizzical. "Spell that out for us, sire," he said. "Why don't we just fan out and beat on every door till we find a good-looking intellectual answering to the name of Steele? Why the special concern?"

"Well, all of the events we've just passed through may turn out to be perfectly casual and easily explained. But we've seen no evidence of this as yet—why have you heard nothing from the woman for two days? Why is a thirty-thousand-dollar car sitting by itself in a country parking lot? It could mean nothing, or it could mean that she has already met with violence from the people she was planning to meet—'lean on' as you, I suspect very appropriately, called it. Or your 'nemesis' woman may have gotten here first. Recall, if Steele found out about those books from her research, the odds are very high it was from research her roommate had already done. Her enemy also thinks she knows where the riches are. No, if there were nothing wrong and she could be discovered by our simply asking around, I think we would have heard from her long since. If, on the other hand, there is some kind of chicanery or even violence going on, we don't know who is our friend or our enemy here.

"Thus the bottom line, as you would say, Steve: I recommend we proceed with care. The question is, how can we start looking over the place and maybe even asking some questions without attracting the attention of some guilty party? For the moment, at least, we're not connected in anyone's mind with the conflict. Query: how can we best blend in?"

"This is an historic site," Crighton replied, "Carson could play the Williamsburg archeologist bit."

Carson said, "You look more like a 'distinguished historian' than any d.h. I ever saw, sir. Want to try a colonial history prof with two graduate students?"

"Thank you," George said. "Another possibility: since most of the strangers on the scene are visiting tourists, we might push that role as far as it would go. Which one do you like best?"

"Tourists are fine by me," Crighton said. "Anybody got a camera?"

Both men shook their heads.

"Not with me," Carson said.

"Wait a minute." Crighton held her photocopies aloft. "We've got a floor plan of the mansion. Want to play old-home buffs? It could get us behind some doors."

"God, and she's got good legs, too," Carson said.

George smiled, "You're right. That is an excellent approach. Let's go with it." He looked at the HABS plan. "That seems to be a guide's house over at the side. It appears to have been an office from the beginning. Let's start there."

The mansion was framed by two one-room brick buildings, perfectly balanced on either side of the stately home in the center. The little building on the right had signs and symbols of the state about it, and they moved toward it across the parking lot.

Carson said, "This was probably a law office in olden time. Lots of the plantations had them. The one at Lee's Stratford looks just like this. Monroe's too. Let me run on ahead."

As they approached the building Carson came out. "An official type at a desk in there says we just missed them. Says to go on up to the house. Wait a minute. They're up on the porch at the mansion. They're waving at us."

A uniformed guide was indeed signaling them to join them, and they waved back and hurried down the oystershell path toward a group of a dozen visitors standing resignedly on the portico.

George set a brisk pace, and as they reached the foot of the steps, Carson gasped, "Jesus. You're in better shape than I am."

George smiled. "I have more time to work on it. Hang in." He raced up the steps and saluted the guide. "Thank you, ma'am, for waiting for us. We are much obliged."

"We're happy to have you join us," she replied, and addressed the larger group. "We are about to go in, and we will be looking at the main floor only. The upstairs rooms are occupied by the family. If you would please wait for me in the great hall in front of you, we can go in now."

She removed a huge brass key from her pocket and inserted it into a polished lock. The group filed through the opened door and dutifully assumed positions around the walls, implying long experience with guided tours. Fully conditioned.

The guide locked the door behind her and leaned on it. "As you can see, this is the center hall, which runs all the way through the house, and the ceiling above the stairs goes all the way to the attic. These open halls are the commonest characteristic of all the great Tidewater homes. They were the air conditioners of their time, and they worked very effectively against the heat of the Virginia summer—which in this area runs well over half of the year," she smiled wryly.

"These great halls were where so much of the daily life of the plantations occurred. All of the doors and windows in the surrounding rooms would be open and the hall would act as a flue—the hot air would rise and bring in outside air to the other rooms. In winter, the halls were the work areas where everyone would come in and take off coats and boots before they entered the carpeted rooms where the fireplaces were.

"This is the room where the children played and the planter talked to his overseers and workmen. You will notice the beautiful sailcloth that covers all of the floor from baseboard to baseboard. This one was painted by two college girls from Annapolis a few years back, and do you notice how well it has held up to all the traffic it gets? The colonial ones worked the same way. They were the equivalent of our linoleum or vinyl. There is one in Kenmore in Fredericksburg that is over a hundred years old, and has lasted incredibly well.

"They used sailcloth since it was durable and woven very wide. The paint is mostly white lead with the pattern painted on in wall colors. This particular design is a copy of the one in the Paca House in Maryland. A sailcloth is laid down and never removed until it has to be replaced.

"The banisters on the stairs are of chestnut from the

surrounding woods, of course. You will notice the various artifacts that have been put in to give the feel of how the center halls were used. Do you see the cradle there? Note the rows of knobs along its rails. They would put the baby in and then take yarn or string and lace it back and forth around the knobs. Then if the cradle fell over, the baby wouldn't fall out.

"The tricorn hat on the peg there is real. Have you ever thought how a tricorn—for three corners, of course— would look flattened out? It's just a round black hat like the Amish wear. They made a tricorn out of it by bending the sides up by hand, steaming it, tying the shape with string, and then drying it in a slow oven. Officers' were made of beaver; ordinary soldiers' were made of wool felt or rabbit fur held together with shellac. When it rained they melted down like the crust on a pie, and had to be done all over again. Let's move on into the dining room now."

She crossed the hall and opened a double door on the left, revealing a high-ceilinged, beautifully furnished room filled with crystal and silver and polished antique furniture.

"Good-looking woman," Carson said, staring at the guide's well-fitted skirt.

"Looking for a knee in the groin?" Crighton asked.

George sighed. "At my age, one is impressed with her professionalism."

"He'd better goddam be impressed with it at his age, too, if he knows what's good for him," Crighton muttered, giving Carson an intense look.

"Strangely enough, the most famous thing about this room," the guide continued, "is the ceiling. It has appeared in numberless books about great American homes. It is carved plaster, and is fully comparable to those that were common in the great houses of England in the 1750s and 60s. It is the original, and has never been touched

97

other than being painted over many times through the past two hundred years.

"It was actually made on the floor here—made of ordinary plaster of Paris and horsehair. It was then lifted up in sections and glued to the overhead plaster and laths with animal-hide glue from the plantation here. The chair cushions, which look like nylon or vinyl, are made from dyed horses' tails. They are the originals, easily wiped clean if anything is spilled on them, and as you can see are still intact after many years of heavy use.

"The table is set for lunch, which was the main meal of the colonies. It would have been eaten at two or three in the afternoon, and there would always have been more food served than could be eaten. There would have been a light supper at about seven o'clock.

"People always ask about the Venetian blinds. Yes, they had Venetian blinds. They were common in Virginia, where they let in the breeze and shielded the room from the hot sun. When Mr. Jefferson moved from the capital, he took all of his with him back to Monticello. Venetian blinds had been common in Europe since the 1300s.

"The Fairfaxes who lived here were real estate developers. The original Lord Fairfax had been given five million empty acres on a tongue of land between the Potomac and the Rappahannock rivers, and the grant ran all the way up to the Blue Ridge Mountains. He sent his cousin over to run the operation, and the cousin built Belvoir to live in. When the lord himself came over from England to see how everything was going, he liked the house and the scene so much he stayed on and never went back. From 1741 to the Revolution this house was both the Fairfax home and the head of their business. The idea was to make as much money out of the land as they could, and just like a developer today, they put in roads and set up their equivalent of shopping centers—the courthouses—to start settlements. They sold farms when they could, rented land when they had to, offered mortgages, and did what they could to make the land attractive. The main office of this enterprise is across the hall, so let's move over to that room there." She motioned to a corner room on the opposite side of the building.

George held back and let the crowd move on. "Crighton, I think it might be tactically wise if you attached yourself to the lady after this is over. Find out as much as you can about the people who live in this place now. From her looks and uniform she appears to be a representative of the state, so she should be fairly detached and reliable. I think Steve and I might concentrate on the building. I'd like to find out if there's any place in it or around it that could hold three thousand books!"

"Let *me* follow the guide, and Crighton can go with you," Carson said.

"Jerk," Crighton snapped. "She's too bright for you. You'd never get to first base. Seriously, you two. Did you look at these HABS plans I've been carrying around all day? Did you notice that half of the area that's under this center hall she's so big on has no doors."

"What are you talking about, woman?"

"Look at it. The shot we copied is the cellar ground plan. Not the first floor. It has four rooms on the sides—each one with a fireplace—and a pantry toward the front. But the back of the center area is completely closed in. No access of any kind. It's twenty-one feet wide and sixteen feet deep. Says so right on the plan. Is that big enough to hold three thousand books?" Crighton handed the Xerox to George.

"Heavens yes," he replied. "With modern floor-to-ceiling shelving, we assume a nine-by-twelve room will hold seven thousand volumes and still have wide enough aisles to shove a book truck through."

"Dammit, woman, you have done it again! You are an endless source of delight. How I do love you. There is

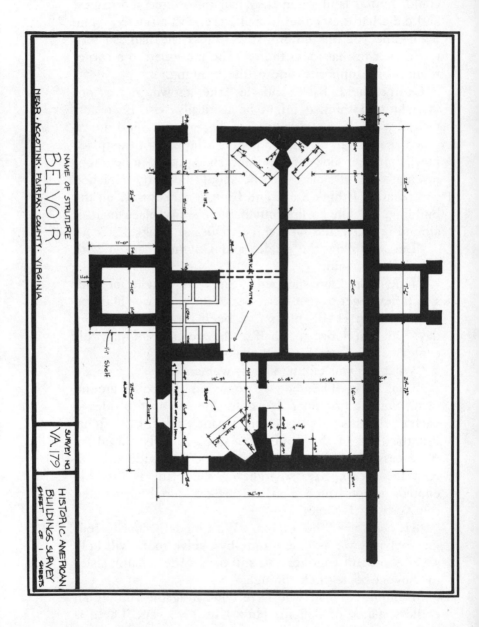

nothing as sexy as an intelligent, beautiful woman. Have I ever—"

"Not now, Carson. Some other time. But don't lose it," she said, "it could be useful on some dull night."

George handed the plan back and said, "The cellar is certainly the place to start. Beautifully done, Crighton. Very observant. We are in your debt. Oops, we'd better catch up with the crowd, they seem to be going out the back door."

The guide was still talking. "I would urge you walk through the gardens between here and the edge of the river. They are believed to be laid out exactly as they were two hundred years ago, since the paths are lined with boxwood that is fully that old. The formal flower beds are copies of traditional English designs. Be careful of the far edge. The lawn drops off pretty abruptly to the Potomac below. There used to be a low brick wall out there, but erosion of the bank dropped it into the river. Oh, the two ladies over there to the right are the current owners of the mansion—the Brents. They are deeply involved in gardening—all over Virginia, as a matter of fact—and I'm sure they'll be happy to answer any questions you might have if you don't take up too much of their time. They're cordial but a little crusty.

"And thank you for visiting Belvoir. I hope you'll come again many times in the future."

George caught Crighton's eye and nodded toward the guide. He tapped his own chest and pointed toward the crusty sisters.

Chapter 14

T HE guide stood to the side of the porch overlooking the garden and watched her latest group of tourists go down the steps and disperse among the various paths and flower beds. Crighton watched her from inside the hall and observed a general softening of carriage and a sigh of fatigue. The guide leaned against a pillar and seemed to coast as one would at the end of a day. Surely there were more tours to be run before the end of her duty, Crighton thought. She stepped down on to the porch and crossed over to where the young woman was standing.

"That was great," Crighton said. "You do that beautifully. How many times a day do folks like us make you go through all that?"

"Thank you. No, I must admit, so far I really haven't gotten tired of it. I do two in the morning and three in the afternoon, and it isn't bad at all."

"How long have you been at it?"

"Almost a year now. I'm really here to work out the take-over of the property by the state. The guiding was sort of a sideline, but it's fun and has let me get to know the family more than I probably would have if I'd just done planning."

"What do you mean, 'take-over'?" Crighton asked.

"The Brents are giving the mansion to the state, and we'll run it along with George Mason's Gunston Hall as a single unit. Gunston is the next plantation down the river. Each one of these necks had its big house on the point and the plantation out behind. The Fairfax's Belvoir was the first, and then Lewis Washington built Mount Vernon on the north and Mason put up Gunston Hall to the south at about the same time. They'll make a nice unit. Mount Vernon will tell the political story, we'll emphasize the land development and colonial economy here, and we hope to do a working colonial farm at Gunston. It really is fascinating."

"I was intrigued that there appeared to be no kitchen in sight here. Was the cooking done in the cellar?" Crighton asked.

"No, colonial cooking was almost always done in a separate building outside. The male writers always say that was because of the danger of fire, but I think they miss the point. The kitchen not only was perpetually hot from the fireplace and the ovens, but it was always smoky and smelled of fat and ashes and general garbage. Not quite the Williamsburg gingerbread bouquet, I suspect," she laughed.

"Was it really women's work?"

"Oh, yes. You never hear of men doing anything except killing poultry and cleaning fish. They helped some with butchering in the fall, but real cooking was invariably done by the women. Come to think of it, there's a modern division of labor there, too. When these men went out to hunt or do military duty, the cooking was done by male servants, and Washington's diaries note pastries and fancy meat dishes, but when they got back home, apparently it never crossed their minds to go into the kitchen. Interesting. There might be a paper in that." She laughed. "Would you like to see the kitchen here? It's opposite the guide office—there by the parking lot."

"I'd love to," Crighton said. "But that puts it in *front* of the house. I assumed the kitchen would be out behind."

"No, that *is* behind. Like Mount Vernon and all the others, the houses faced the river. That's where practically everybody came from—and it was specially so with Belvoir. Lord Fairfax got Belvoir made the custom house for the whole of northern Virginia. Anything shipped in or out had to stop here and get the paperwork done. The Custom House sat by the dock down below the garden cliff."

"Is the Custom House reconstructed, too?"

"No, it's long since been eroded away. The shoreline was a full city block farther out toward Maryland in those days." The guide smiled and said cordially, "And don't let the Brents hear you say 'reconstructed.' The ladies would chew you up. Williamsburg was mostly restored and reconstructed. Belvoir is the very original, untouched, real thing."

Crighton put a hand across her face in mock embarrassment. "Forgive me, I knew not what I said. I take it the Brents are still in residence."

"Oh, yes. Sarah and Martha are very much *in situ,* and we've also got a nephew here. They live on the second floor."

"Isn't that pretty unlikely?"

"Not in Virginia. You've heard of Shirley Plantation on the James? The ruling member of the Carter-Hill family lives there—the tenth generation, would you believe it? There still are Tayloes at Mount Airy and Landon Carters at Sabine Hall—the families have been there uninterruptedly since the 1600s. Just marvelous."

"What are the Brents like?"

"Well, it's really rather astonishing to find people like

104

them in this country. I guess being a Rockefeller or an Adams might be the same, but the Brents know they are twelfth generation. Everything they do or say or think has that knowledge behind it. Most of us worry about what's going to happen to us or what people think about us or what we ought to do in a situation either so we won't get into trouble or so we'll get promoted or something, but they never seem to ask any of these questions. They're Brents. That takes care of everything."

Crighton and the guide had gone around the house and come out onto the oystershell walk in back. The kitchen building, now on their right, was a mirror image of the law office on the left. The distance between the support buildings and the mansion surprised Crighton.

"Do you mean they carried food all the way from there to here?"

"Every step in winter and rain. It probably wasn't so bad in summer, but it must have been hell the rest of the time. All the serving dishes had double bottoms and they'd put hot water in them, but even if it helped the food it made them harder to carry. Really amazing. Do you know the Virginia houses?"

"Yes, I'm about a sophomore-level old-house buff. I've done Williamsburg and the Washington and Lee homes and Monticello."

"Right. Well, you know every one of those have kitchens yards away. Stratford and the Governor's Palace and Kenmore are a real trek even in good weather."

"Is the nephew you mentioned the head of the family?"

"Hardly. He's an exceedingly unpleasant young character who's barely tolerated by the ladies. Martha and Sarah run the Brents with an iron hand. Not only the house but the finances. They're leading a stockholder's attack on Commonwealth Coal and Shipping right now." The guide smiled as she strode toward the red brick building.

"They don't need money, then?"

"Not hardly."

"What motivates them? Wanting to get richer?"

"No, I think their wealth is simply part of being a Brent. Just like the preacher's wife is expected to help with church suppers, being a Brent means you serve on boards. They have a very clear-cut set of principles concerning what's expected. I don't think I'd ever thought of that before, but most of us keep asking ourselves, 'What should I do with this situation?' They seem to ask, 'What shouldn't we do? What is not acceptable?' That's very interesting. I've never considered that, but it's true: when I ask them questions about the transfer or the future of the place, they never reply with a pragmatic decision—what would work best—but with almost a . . . a . . . protocol one. What is expected?"

"Expected by whom?"

The guide laughed. "I don't know. God, maybe. No, that's not true. It's all the old Virginians. What would the other F.F.V.s expect."

Crighton felt an involuntary chill.

"Doesn't the nephew have the same rules?" she asked.

"They seem to have missed him completely, now that you mention it. He trusts no one, has a very low opinion of himself and everybody else, and he is acutely aware of money. I don't know why the family code failed to take him with it. And here we are," she said, approaching the little building. "Go right in, it isn't locked. In fact, we usually try to keep the door open so people will go in on their own. I wonder who closed it now?"

They entered the usual plantation kitchen with a huge fireplace at one end, herbs, corn, and preserved fowl hanging from the rafters, and a long, well-rubbed worktable down the center of the room. It all smelled dry, dusty, and, Crighton thought, surprisingly like the cellar in a brownstone row house.

106

"Do you want the tour or a little peace and quiet?" the guide asked.

"Well, I don't want to take up too much of your time, but—"

"I'll give you the ten-cent headlines. You can come back and get the full five-dollar treatment some other time." The guide smiled and sat down at the end of one of the benches. "The fireplace is the big thing here. The moral equivalent of our ranges, of course, and the point of it all.

"The old cooks developed a marvelous skill at using the coals off a log to do everything we do, and apparently it was all reactive . . . unconscious. They knew just how much and how bright the coals had to be to warm something, or broil it, or bake it, and when you interview hill folk about it nowadays, they can't even think of how to say it, much less have any formula or recipe.

"When the kitchen was in use, they'd bring in a large log and lay it across those iron dogs in back, getting it burning from yesterday's coals, and then that log would be kept smoldering all day long. When they wanted to cook something, they'd knock coals off it and drag the coals up front with those long-handled scrapers there. The pots sat on little trivets that you'd set over the coals. A cook would have half a dozen of these little mounds burning at the same time. She could tell by the glow when to bring on new coals or blow on the old ones.

" 'Most everything was cooked in kettles. There'd be a huge one full of hot water hanging down from a hook, and lots of smaller ones around. There were lots of stews and boiled meat. Every few meals they'd broil some meat on skewers, and these would be set in front of the main log and either turned by a kid or a ratchet-and-weight arrangement. They'd very carefully catch the melted fat in a drip pan and make gravy and *soap* out of it! They made all their soap themselves, of course, and they made it by pouring the fat into a barrel full of wood ashes. What they got really was 'soapy,' but it never hardened—it was like soft paste, and it was used mostly for washing clothes. Pots and pewter were 'scrubbed' after every meal with plain wood ashes right out of the fireplace."

She turned slightly and pointed to an opening in the brick flue. "Baking was mostly done in a covered pot—a Dutch oven—but the big plantations also had ovens like that one on the side. They'd put live coals in it in the morning and heat up the bricks and then scrape the coals out and put in the bread or pie dough and let it bake overnight. They got a crust that was thicker and harder than ours, but it tasted better. They put honey on it. Rarely butter."

Crighton said, "You say it tasted better. Have you actually done it yourself?"

"Oh, yes. I've tried to do everything I've talked about. I spent a couple of weeks in the highlands behind Bristol, where there are still folks cooking in open fireplaces."

"Great Scott! How did you find them?"

The guide laughed. "Only in America. They have been so heavily researched by the folklorists that there are directories of them at the State Historical Society. I sometimes think the mountain people make most of their living letting people like us live with them 'before the old ways die out.' They're wonderful folks, though. They got so much fun out of watching me kill and butcher a hog I thought they should have paid *me* for the trip!"

"Then most of our knowledge of how the kitchens were back then comes from modern, leftover traditions now?"

"Only part. The colonial kitchen has been well researched, and oddly enough it is one of our best dating devices. They actually did burn down fairly frequently, and when we dig them we can spot a lot of clues. You can date things by the size of the hole in pipestems. Noel Hume at Williamsburg has a whole system on this. You can tell age by the kind of glaze on plates and serving dishes."

"One last thing and I'll let you go. You always see the dining rooms dressed for a fancy banquet. What was a plain, ordinary breakfast in the old days?"

"Breakfast was served about ten o'clock, although everybody got up with the sun. They'd drink a glass of beer or cider and go out and work for three or four hours. Then when they came in for the midmorning meal they'd have mush or griddle cakes with *boiled* bacon—not fried—and all of this would be washed down with more beer. They rarely drank water and not much milk either. They suspected that these made them sick, and they were right too much of the time. We take so much for granted today."

Crighton stood up and turned toward the door.

"This has been just great. I must let you get back to your work now, but I will indeed come back for that five-dollar tour sometime. Thank you so much."

"My pleasure."

They started out the door together and Crighton turned toward the parking lot before her.

The guide asked, "Are you going to your car or are you joining your friends at the house? I can show you a shortcut to the gardens, if you're headed that way."

"No, I'll wait at the car. By the way, we're parked by a magnificent Porsche out there. Do you know who it belongs to? Is it one of your Brents'?"

"Where is that?" the guide asked.

"There at the back beside—"

She stopped. Carson's car was where they had left it. A half-dozen tourists' cars were in the row nearest the house, but the remainder of the lot was quite empty. The red sports car had disappeared completely.

Damnation! she thought. Now what?

Aloud she said, "Maybe I will go back to the gardens. How were you going to send me?"

Chapter 15

CRIGHTON hurried toward the front of the mansion as quickly as she could walk without breaking into an outright run.

Jesus, what a mess, she thought. Durance was probably headed toward her own apartment and could walk right into having her throat cut, completely unaware of all their attempts to warn her. Worse yet, she might head back to Charlottesville and walk into even more trouble at U. Va. Dammit, why had this possibility never occurred to any of them?

Increasingly breathless, she rounded the corner of the house and looked across the garden. Nobody. Not George, not the women, not even any tourists. She ran up the steps of the front porch to get some height, and although she could now see down onto the pattern of the boxwood hedges and even to the edge of the drop-off to the river, there was no one in sight. She swore again with deepening conviction. Where is everybody? And where has Durance been for the past two days, yet? This is maddening, and we haven't got time to stand around and talk about it.

She tried the door back into the house, and found it predictably locked. She beat on it with increasing frustration, but got no response. She ran down the steps of the porch and outright sprinted around the opposite side of the building to what she now perceived as the rear of the mansion, to find most of the remaining cars in the lot driving away. No sign of either George or Carson, and no sign of the guide either. Reluctant as she was to blow what little cover they had, she decided that she was going to have to get to a phone, and she could think of only two options for finding one. She could drive back to the highway and look for a gas station or a convenience store, or she could throw secrecy to the winds and go into the guide's house. The first choice took care of itself; she had no key to Carson's car. She looked at it now sitting almost alone on the asphalt. So near and so damn far, she thought.

She had now reached the guide's room, and after a second's hesitation burst in. There was a pale, very neat man sitting at a desk with a calculator and ledgers spread before him. If he only had steel-rimmed glasses, he'd be the perfect bookkeeper, Crighton thought.

To her astonishment, he picked up a pair of steel-rimmed glasses and set them carefully on his nose. "May I help you?"

"I'm desperately in need of a telephone. Is there a pay phone anywhere around here?"

"There's one in the rest-rooms on the other side of the mansion. It's in the old school house. If it's an emergency—and not too far—you could use that one." He pointed toward a phone sitting on the other desk in the room. The desk presumably belonged to the missing guide.

She weighed loss of privacy against loss of time and said, "Thank you so much. It *is* an emergency and it's just to Washington. Would that be okay?"

"Go ahead."

She lifted the phone as she dropped into the empty chair. Fast work with the system got her the District police department and, to her immense relief, Lieutenant Conrad. Somewhat breathlessly, she brought him up to date on the situation and ended by saying, "So you can see, we're losing control. Do you have any idea how we can warn the woman that she may be walking into real trouble—like being cut down by her own roommate, for one possibility?"

Conrad took his usual three-beat pause before answering, and then said, "Yeah, Miss Jones, I think you're right. We shouldn't take any more chances. I'll get a car out to your apartment, and I think I'd better call U. Va. security and have them look around down there. You're out of my jurisdiction where you are now, of course, but I think I'd better alert the Fairfax County department—"

"Wait a minute, this place is either owned by the state of Virginia or is about to be. The guide wears a Virginia uniform. Does that make any difference?"

"You mean use the state patrol? Okay, that might actually be faster. They could alert their cars on the interstates. All right. We'll skip the county for now. How do I get back to you?"

"Look, so far nobody here knows what we're up to and—"

"That's a luxury you won't have much longer," Conrad said casually.

"I know, but I need to talk to Dr. George and Steve. Could I call you back in just a few minutes?"

"Have it your way. I'll start the APB rolling and place a few calls down the line."

"Bless you. I'll be calling you back in minutes . . . I hope."

They parted, and Crighton wondered why she felt no sense of relief. Shared responsibility should have eased her usual hovering guilt about everything. Instead, she wondered if she had not started them all down a slide toward real disaster.

She suddenly remembered the bookkeeper, who had been diligently keying his calculator throughout the conversation.

"Thank you again. Really," she said.

He nodded without looking up or meeting her eyes. She bit her lip and headed for the door.

Chapter 16

THE reason Crighton had been unable to find George was that he was at that moment walking with the sisters along the shore of the Potomac fifty feet below the lip of the garden cliff. He was, he believed, working very hard trying to step on the places where the wet ground looked more like sand than mud while simultaneously trying to probe the Brent sisters' purpose in life. His prime target was to determine whether the Steele woman had contacted the sisters yet, and if so, whether they were antagonists or allies. Had she indeed attempted to "lean on" these intriguing women, and if so how would they—or how *had* they—responded? It was taking all of George's concentration to hit all of his targets simultaneously.

It had started a short time before in the garden itself. He had ingratiated himself rather skilfully, he thought, by complimenting them on the beauty of the gardens, then asking what he hoped were thoughtful questions about the authenticity of the design of the beds, and finally he had made insightful observations about the sophistication of the original occupants of the mansion. This, at last, had flushed out the theme he'd been probing for and set the conversation down the path he hoped might be productive.

Sarah Brent had replied, "Yes, indeed. The juxtaposition of cultures is very difficult for us to imagine even from this short distance." She had looked back toward the mansion. "When the house was built, you could reach country that was completely controlled by Indians in a single day, and in three days you could reach valleys that had never been seen by a white man. Yet Lord Fairfax was writing about hearing Bach at Williamsburg, he'd been reading *Tom Jones,* and his brother replied he'd heard Handel's *Messiah* before he took ship to Virginia. The music is almost exactly as old as the house. William Fairfax was very sensitive to music, but Thomas could barely carry a tune."

"Were the Brents sympathetic to the Fairfaxes?" George asked.

"When?"

"At the Revolution. When the Brents took over the house."

"Oh, yes. They were all good friends. George William—Washington's friend—went back to England, and his cousin Thomas, who carried the title, moved inland to the Shenandoah Valley to wait for the war to end. The property was empty for a very short time and then it was advertised for sale, and William—William Brent, that is—bought it. The advertisement was written by Washington himself, and the money was later paid to the Fairfaxes as a result of a case brought by John Marshall. They were all friends."

"It's wonderful how you clearly know them as real people."

"Oh, it hasn't been that long ago. Josephine Tey reminds us how these people overlap without our thinking about it. She points out that it was possible for an ordinary

115

Englishman to have seen both Elizabeth I and George I—in the flesh. One of our family could have known Lord Fairfax and Henry Ford, you know." She laughed. "A person could have talked to Mr. Jefferson and seen a very young Ronald Reagan, as far as that goes."

"Really, is that possible?"

"Of course, Adams and Mr. Jefferson died in 1826, a person could have talked to them and seen the Wright Brothers fly their plane, read Einstein's theory of relativity, met Freud." She laughed, evidently pleased with the thought. George could not resist it. "I notice you refer to Mr. Jefferson but not Mr. Adams. Has the family not forgiven the Northerner?"

"It wasn't that he was from the North. It was simply that he made life very difficult for Mr. Jefferson. Mr. Jefferson was thinking of the country's welfare and what was good for everyone. Adams was interested only in lining the pockets of his friends the industrialists at the expense of everyone else."

"But Jefferson forgave Adams at the end."

"Yes, he was a marvelously generous character. He was often too good for his own good."

"Are the Brents related to the Jeffersons?"

"Not blood kin. The families knew each other throughout much of the last century, but I can't think of any marriages. Can you, Martha?"

"No. Certainly not in the colonial period. Maybe antebellum. The Jefferson line is not so obvious since the name died out so quickly. The two daughters married Randolphs and Eppeses, and there were no sons, of course. Martha died when Lucy was born." Martha Brent threw this out casually, as if any intelligent person would have known it already.

"I presume those early years were particularly hard on women," George said.

"How hard?" Sarah snapped.

"Well, the constant work and the dangers of childbirth, among other things," George said with surprise.

"Nonsense," Sarah replied. "The women of the aristocracy had a very satisfying life, and death through childbirth was no more frequent than death from typhoid and dysentery and who knew what else for the men. There are just as many examples of women having two and three husbands as there are of men with successive wives. Hmmph! The great concentrations of land almost all came through the women. Martha Dandridge was the wealthiest person in Virginia when she married George Washington—she owned over seventeen thousand acres and was worth nearly half a million dollars in cash. She'd picked it up playing widow along the way. Almost all of the Lee land came through the women. All of them went through two or three husbands at a minimum, accumulating property as they went. But the men were always off politicking or in some war or other. This left the women to run the land like it should be. The wife running the plantation during the War between the States was simply doing what she'd been doing ever since colonial times. It was a good thing too. Men always make decisions for the immediate present; women think a generation ahead—or more."

By this time the women had led George out of the garden and down a sloping path to the river shore below. He sensed that his footing, both on the ground and in the conversation, was getting perilous. He tried changing the subject.

"Is that Gunston Hall there?" He pointed through the trees to a headland a half-mile down the Potomac.

"Yes," Martha Brent replied. "They're going to link Belvoir to it and run the two as a single site. We're giving the mansion to the state."

"I presume this is going to be very difficult for you."

"No, I think we'll both find a considerable relief. We are acutely conscious of being just the present occupants

117

of a family tradition that is now nearly three hundred years old. We rarely can do anything with our lives or money or property without asking, 'What would *they* have wanted us to do?' It will be nice to hand this part of the patrimony over to the community."

"Do you feel it belongs to everybody and that they should assume the care for it?"

"No. We assume it belongs to the Brents and everybody should see how certain standards and principles have worked for a dozen generations. It is a model for the community to emulate."

Sensing his batting average was nearing zero, he stumbled grimly on. "What happens to all the furnishings? Will you take them with you, or do they stay with the mansion?"

"The furnishings are as much a part of the mansion as the walls and ceilings. Everything stays except our clothing and the electrical appliances."

"Is the upstairs filled with antiques like those wonderful things we see on the first floor?"

"No."

Oh what the hell, he thought. "What's in the cellar? How is it arranged?"

That apparently did it. There was no answer at all; the query seemed to have been lost in the damp air. At this point the rough path they were following under the overhang of the bluff turned abruptly up a creek bed and rose to the far side of the garden above. In dramatic contrast to the manicured lawns, the creek sides were filled with dense underbrush, the footing was moist from recent rains, and a general sense of disappearing into the uncut frontier prevailed.

George accepted the increased incline as a convenient excuse for letting the conversation die. They thus walked in deliberate silence until they reached the top, where the land flattened out and the light reappeared overhead.

George looked around to get his bearings and discovered the house farther off to the right than he had expected it to be. He saw Crighton Jones as a miniature figure waving frantically from the top steps of the front porch. Wild arm movements appeared to be instructing him to head directly for the parking lot, which lay on a broad diagonal from where he was now following the women.

He sighed and improvised a farewell, which the Brent sisters barely acknowledged. Setting out on a course that would converge with Crighton's hurried walk, he had almost reached shouting distance when the police car burst down the entry way and roared into sight. There was no siren but it carried wildly flashing lights and came to a TV fishtail stop.

So much for the quiet undercover approach, George thought. Now what?

Chapter 17

CRIGHTON and George converged at the edge of the parking lot, both headed for the police car.

"Bad news," Crighton said. "The Porsche has disappeared—apparently while we were all inside. I panicked and called Conrad. I thought he'd better get someone out to the apartment to be sure Steele wasn't ambushed on the way in." She gasped for breath but kept on walking. "Conrad was going to tell the state police to cover the roads back to U. Va., but he didn't say anything about sending a cop here."

"You didn't panic. Sounds like good sense to me. Well handled." George was also getting winded, but added, "And I certainly wasn't getting anywhere with my approach."

The officer had gotten out of the patrol car and was coming toward them.

"Are you Miss Jones?"

Crighton introduced George and before she could pose any questions to the officer, he answered them.

"My name is Park. Your friend in Washington apparently thought we should find out what was happening here. I understand you were concerned about a friend or acquaintance or someone who was being threatened. They put out an all-points bulletin about the car, and it's been found."

"What!" Crighton shouted. "That's not possible. I couldn't have called it in over thirty minutes ago. They must have confused it with something else."

"No, I think not. I just got the report as I came in here. They found it in the most obvious place—it's at National Airport. Been there about an hour. The airport security picked it up on the first pass after the APB. Nobody in it; they're checking with the airlines. Do you have any idea where she'd be most likely to go?"

Crighton held on to the top of her head. "I can't stand it! What in the name of God is going on?"

"Yeah," Park said. "I could use a little background myself. What *is* going on here?"

George said, "May I suggest we adjourn to the guide's building?"

They marched grimly to the little brick office, and Park moved in as if commandeering enemy territory.

"Who are you?" he said to the man with the calculator.

"Norman Phelps. I keep the fiscal records. Can I be of help?"

"Who do you work for?"

"The Brents."

"Okay. We'll be needing the use of your office."

"Do you want me to leave?"

"Suit yourself." He turned to Crighton, but George started talking before the officer could control the questions. The bookkeeper tried to look like a part of the furniture and succeeded so well that everyone forgot he was there.

"The situation is like this," George said briskly. "Miss Jones there works for the Werner-Bok research library in

Washington. For professional reasons, she offered to board a visiting scholar whom she had never met, until the person could make other housing arrangements. The woman was named . . ." he looked at Crighton.

"Durance Steele."

"I don't know why I have so much trouble with that name," George said with a frown. "Is it senility or Freud? Anyway, the woman left on a day's trip to get revenge—her characterization—for some indignity she had suffered as a student at the University of Virginia. Two things then occurred: she did not return to the apartment, and Miss Jones received a threatening phone call and then a mailed note saying that some woman was going to kill her. Steele, not Jones."

The state trooper seemed to be following the story, but began to register a growing skepticism.

"Miss Jones called on a friend of hers and myself for aid and comfort in the situation, and we set out to find the missing woman. By a process of elimination based on some hints she had let fall, we came out here and discovered her rather unusual car parked in the parking lot. While we were all preoccupied looking over the mansion, she drove the car away before we could warn her of the danger she was in."

"How do you know she was driving it?" Park asked.

"Well, I guess we don't, literally. Are you suggesting that someone stole it or something?"

"No, I'm just following your original thought. If someone was out to kill the woman, she could have been killed here, and the car could have been moved to throw everyone off."

George smiled and nodded. "Well taken. We had reason to think that the Steele woman was seeking something of value here, and I suspect we both assumed that she'd gotten money or was going off to get money or something. Your observation is precisely correct. We don't

122

know if she was in the car. Of course, technically we don't know she was in the car when it came here in the first place, but we don't have any reason not to think so."

"Where is the third person in your party?"

"Good question. Crighton, where is Steve? Do you know?"

"I thought he was with you. I haven't seen him since the tour."

"No, I went off to where the Brent women were and he disappeared behind my back."

They both went to a window to look out, and Crighton said, "There. There he is. He's coming around the far side of the house. He's with another guy."

George opened the back door of the office, and the officer went through with all but Phelps following. The two groups met halfway between the buildings.

"Great! A cop! Just what I needed," the other man said. He was half shoving and half urging Carson ahead of him. Carson was wearing a broad smile and was projecting an air of something-attempted-something-done.

"Who are you?" Park asked.

"Elliott Brent. I live here."

Crighton looked at Carson and signaled "What?" with her eyebrows.

Carson beamed. "The nephew. Towering figure."

Brent shot him a glance approaching hatred and said, "I caught the son-of-a-bitch prying a window open. Lock him up. We'll throw the book at him. Breaking and entering."

"Where was this window?" Park asked.

"At the main house. The cellar."

Crighton and George fixed their eyes on Carson with great interest and Carson smiled again. "Sorry. Didn't have time to find out anything. Renfrew here came down like the wolf on the fold."

"Is this the third member of your party?" Park asked George.

"That's correct. That is Dr. Stephen Carson. He's an archeologist at Williamsburg," George said, thinking that he'd given him as much respectability as was possible with one sentence.

"What *were* you doing?" Park asked Carson.

"Essentially just what he said," Carson replied, "except I wasn't going to enter, just break. We're missing a woman, among other things, and nobody would let me go down into that cellar to see if she was there. They've got these colonial bars over the windows, and I was merely trying to adjust some so I could see in better when the frame came off. Renfrew here didn't give me a chance to explain."

"Where were you headed now?" Park asked Brent.

"I was going to hand him over to Fairchild to call the cops."

"Who's Fairchild?"

"The symbol of the state here. Grace Fairchild. Curator, site historian, guide. Whatever they call her. She's got a uniform. Authority."

"You all seem to think the cellar might relate to the missing woman. I think I'd like to look in it myself. Mr. Brent, will you take us there, please?"

"No. You're goddam right I won't. What do you think you're doing breaking into a private home? You're fucking-A not going in there without a warrant or something more impressive than just a 'let me see it, please.' Jesus Christ! What an asshole."

Park looked at him with more contempt than irritation and said, "Frankly I'm not sure who owns the house at this moment, but as long as you have a Virginia state sign at the gate, and you are getting state police protection, we will assume that the state owns it. We will look at the details later. Move it. Where's the door to the place? Is there an outside entrance?"

Elliott Brent assumed an appearance of near-desperation. He managed to place himself between the house and the four persons whom he seemed to perceive as his enemies and stretched out his arms as if to hold them back.

"Wait a minute. Wait a minute," he bleated. "If you're looking for something funny, I'll tell you where to look. Wednesday night there were lights in that building right behind you for half the night." He pointed over their shoulders at the guide's office. "I didn't know who or what was going on, but you ought to look there first."

"What did you think was going on?" Park asked.

"I don't have the slightest idea, but it wasn't usual."

"Is there a guard here at night?"

"No. Fairchild's the guard. If she needs help she calls somebody."

"Does she live here?"

"No, she leaves at six. Comes back at nine in the morning."

"Did you tell anybody about what you saw?"

"No. I thought it would explain itself. It wasn't till you all were bitching about some woman that it occurred to me."

"So what are we to look for?" Park said with increasing distaste.

"I don't know. Let's look around. Maybe somebody put something in there."

The group had now started back toward the little brick building, but as they neared the door everyone but Brent stopped and looked at it.

"Why didn't you report this to the curator?"

"Well, frankly, at the time I thought she was the one messing around."

"When was all this?"

"Middle of the night."

"Why did you think it was her?"

"Well, I think I saw somebody that looked like her come across from the cliff."

"I thought you said you hadn't seen anyone."

"Well, I really hadn't. It's just a feeling. I'd been waked up and I wasn't paying that close attention. Remember, it was dark as hell. The only lights were from the windows here."

Park gave him a look that was just short of actionable and started walking slowly around the outside of the building, keeping a distance from the walls but stopping opposite each of the various windows and the front and back doors. Carson followed at a discreet distance while the others waited. Carson could see no sign of disturbed earth except much scuffing in the oystershell walks both front and back.

"Stay here," Park said to the group, and went in. Phelps came hurrying out and joined the silent group looking at the building. Park was gone for several moments, and then came to the entrance.

"There's a loft with a sliding door in it. Would someone steady a chair for me?" he said.

Both Carson and Brent stepped forward, but Brent shouldered his way in front, apparently representing the "owners" in his mind. Carson was not deterred and followed close behind.

Once inside, Brent stepped back against a wall, suddenly assuming a passive role leaning against a window frame. He looks like Mommy who knows where the Easter eggs are and can we find them? thought Carson.

Park glanced at Carson and smiled grimly. "There's nothing in this room but the two desks and the filing cabinets. I pulled all the drawers. They're unlocked, but there's nothing inside but papers. That seems to leave the

126

attic." He looked up at a wooden sliding door in the plastered ceiling.

"I'll get a chair," Carson said, assessing the two rolling office chairs behind the desks. Both looked too small, too unstable, and too mobile. Feeling that one was as dangerous as the other, he selected the nearest, rolled it between the desks, and positioned it below the access panel in the ceiling. "I'll hold it as best I can."

"Umm," said Park, measuring the height between the chair and the sliding door with his eye, "not high enough." He looked around the room and said, "Give me a hand with a desk."

They moved the chair aside and shoved the guide's desk under the hole. The officer climbed on and, by stretching to his full height, got the door lifted up and shoved aside. He frowned and pulled himself into the attic space with an athletic chin-up. After some twisting about he dropped back on to the desk.

"Nothing," he said. "Bare rafters, wooden laths, dust. Nothing else." He looked toward Brent. "So what did you expect?"

Brent shrugged without moving away from the wall. "I've no idea."

"I don't think we can pursue this any further until the Fairchild woman comes back," Park said. "Let's go look at the cellar like you suggested." He nodded toward the desk to ask for Carson's help in returning it to its original position, walking around behind it to help pull it back into place. As he stood behind it he looked down and said irritably, "Wait a minute. Here's another door."

Brent did not move, but Carson joined the officer and they stared down at a trap door, flush with the flooring and made of the same wide, worn planks. It normally would have fallen precisely within the knee-hole of the desk.

Park sighed and dropped down beside it. There was

no hardware apparent, no hinges or handles but a worn finger hole drilled through on one side. Park gingerly reached through the hole and started to lift the panel out of its recess. The door tilted up with surprising ease and Carson helped him lift it out and lean it against the other desk.

They both dropped to their knees and looked into the darkened space. The dusty earth was two feet below them, and lying across it was a body wrapped in black plastic trash bags.

"Damn," said Park. He looked directly at Brent, still leaning passively against the wall, and said harshly, "Get out. You'd better go too," he said to Carson without rancor. "I'll have to check this out first. I'll be out in a minute. Don't anybody go anywhere." He turned back to the hole as Carson followed Brent back into the sunlit yard.

"What?" George asked quietly.

"Not good," Carson said. "There's a body under the floorboards. I'm afraid we've found our lady."

Crighton covered her mouth, and everyone stared silently at the door. Eventually Park reappeared.

"I'm sorry to report," he said in obvious distress, "I'm afraid it's the woman." He looked toward Carson. "I've torn the plastic back and . . . I hate to do this, but someone's got to look down there and tell me if you recognize the person." He looked back and forth between George and Carson, clearly hoping they would volunteer.

"I'm sorry," George said, "but neither Steve nor I have seen Miss Steele. Crighton, could you tell us what to look for?"

Crighton was clenching her teeth so hard the cords of her jaw muscles were outlined, but she said deliberately, "No. I've got to do it. Let me go in. I can . . . I can handle it."

Park stepped back and Crighton marched solemnly through the door and looked into the open hole. She knelt down, flinched, and half averted her eyes, but said clearly, "That is Durance Steele." Rather than looking away, she stared intently into the crawl space as if fixed, and then suddenly, to George and Carson's astonishment, shouted, "Damn her! Damn her, damn her."

"The body in the hole?" Park asked in confusion.

"No! The woman who did it. The one I talked to. The one who wrote the note. She was ahead of us all the way. You've got to get her before she gets away. The airport—find out where she's going and grab her before she gets off the plane!"

"So what's her name?" Park asked.

Everyone exchanged glances, and Carson put an arm around Crighton. She answered bitterly. "We don't know. All we know is that she used to be Durance Steele's roommate. That is Durance Steele down there and it must have been the roommate who did it. You must not let her get away with this. You've got to find out who she was and go after her at once. Call U.Va., they should know. Apparently they were both well known down there. God damn her! What a waste. What an outrage."

"All right," Park said. "Everybody out. All of you. Quickly, please. I've got some calls to make."

He walked toward the desk and the others filed out the door.

Chapter 18

CARSON and George were staring intently at Crighton Jones, more concerned about how she was dealing with the shock of the developments, than concentrating on the ramifications of the violent death in the building behind them.

Crighton was organizing reality.

"We've got to do something about that poor guide. She's real quality stuff and we can't have her breezing in here to find she's got a nightmare under her own floorboards. What time is it? She must be about due out from her last tour. Should we go find her or wait for her to come here?"

"What do you care?" Elliott Brent asked. "She's paid by the month. It's no skin off her teeth—unless she did it herself."

Crighton looked at him with such fury that George stepped in hastily, more for Crighton's sake than for the nephew's. "Has there ever been a murder in the Brent family history?"

"Hell, I suppose so," Brent answered. "The early ones had more than their share of bloodiness. Some of our finest names had slaughter on their hands. The sainted Wythe was poisoned by his nephew. Two of the Randolphs killed somebody each. Hell, they were all so interbred it's a wonder they weren't completely certifiable. Do you know about the glory days of the Republic when we had giants in the land?

"Speaking of Randolphs, do you know about Big Bill Randolph of Turkey Island? What a hoot! He started it all by marrying Mary Isham of Bermuda Hundred on the James. They had five sons. The first one was called Isham and he had a daughter who had a son—Thomas Jefferson, president of the United States. The second son was called John—he got himself knighted so he's in the books as Sir John. He had a son who had a son—Edmund Randolph, first attorney general of the U.S. and secretary of state under Washington. The third son was called Thomas. He had a daughter, who had a daughter, who had a son—John Marshall, founding chief justice of the Supreme Court. The fourth son was called William after the old man. He had a daughter who had a daughter who had a son, Light-Horse Henry Lee, aide-de-camp to Washington, governor of Virginia—and father of Robert E. Lee. The fifth son was called Richard who had a son who had a son—John Randolph of Roanoke, leader of the Republicans in the House of Representatives, and enormous wheel in both Richmond and Washington. Ha! Did you know that Jefferson and Randolph and Marshall and Lee were all fucking cousins, for Chrissake? It's the God's truth. Talk about nepotism! My sacred ass. A real meritocracy! Everybody had an equal chance so long as they had the right name when they applied for the vacancy!" He shook his head, beaming with delight.

"Is that true?" George asked Carson.

Carson smiled. "I'd never really thought it out, but when he says it that way, I think it is. For nearly two hundred years Virginia was run by three hundred families—almost exactly three hundred, as a matter of fact. That's the number of plantations that completely filled up the Tidewater. But I'd forgotten or never really thought about the Randolphs having such a corner on the leadership. They did manage to dominate the market, didn't they?"

Brent looked at Phelps and said, "Hey! It's the company clerk! Heady times, eh Norm? A body right under your floor! That ought to steam up your glasses."

Phelps looked more frightened than angry, but before he could reply the officer came out of the house and joined them. "They're sending some plainclothes people over from the barracks at Fredericksburg. It'll take them about twenty minutes. We might save them some time if you'd give me some feel about where everybody was."

"Do you have any idea when the body might have been put in there?" George asked.

"No more than you do." He turned toward Brent, "All these lights and things in the night were last night were they?"

"No. Night before last. Wednesday."

"Was there any activity earlier in the week?"

"I wouldn't know. I went to New York last Friday and didn't come back till Wednesday night."

"What were you doing in New York?"

"Business."

"Would there be someone to verify your time?"

"For every day—and different people, too."

"And last night? Was there any activity last night around here?"

"I didn't see anything one way or the other. I watched television and went to bed."

"Anyone see you?"

"Sarah and Martha sat right beside me."

Park turned to George. "When did you get here?"

"We must have arrived a little after eleven this morning. We'd just missed the start of the eleven o'clock tour and the guide waited for us at the house."

132

"Did you all come together?"

"Yes. In that car you can see at the rear of the parking lot."

"Had you ever been here before—any of you?"

They all shook their heads, and George said, "No, this was the first time for all of us, and it was almost a fluke that we came when we did. We were using the parking lot to turn around in, in anticipation of going to a different place when we noticed Miss Steele's car."

"The one at the airport."

"Yes."

Throughout this discussion Crighton had been looking back toward the house, eager to intercept the guide before she blundered into what was clearly going to be a stress-ridden responsibility for her once the police arrived in force. Crighton had taken an instant dislike to Elliott Brent and was eager to warn the guide about the casual way Brent was placing her under suspicion with the police. Crighton was intrigued with her own reaction. She recognized how quickly she had identified with Grace Fairchild. She suspected it was not only the fact that they had similar relationships to the public institutions they served, but she had quickly sensed a shared set of values and attitudes toward both the public and their work. As she had said, Fairchild had quality, and giving her a chance to know what had been said behind her back before the authorities arrived seemed the least Crighton could offer. She casually pulled back from Park, drawing George and Carson with her.

"Hey, you guys," she said in a low voice, "I think I'm going back to bring that woman up to date. If you can keep the cop distracted, I'll act like I'm going to the car and loop around behind to the house."

The men nodded agreement, and George stepped toward the officer while Crighton pantomimed a search for something in her purse, and then distractedly walked toward the car without bothering to ask permission.

"Who will they send to you?" George asked.

"Oh, we've got a scene-of-the-crime unit running off of LEA funds—the van and technicians and so forth. They spend most of their time on highway accidents and farm break-ins, so they'll go for this in a big way."

Crighton could be seen making a wide arc behind the officer's back and disappearing behind the kitchen building.

"They might actually leave it in my hands," Park continued. "I've done some investigation work."

"Will you need us to stay here?" George asked.

"Why, where do you want to go?"

"Well, actually we need to get back to Washington as quickly as possible."

"Will that Washington lieutenant vouch for you?"

"Oh, yes, I think he can lodge the proper bonafides."

"In that case, so long as we get all the details of what you know before you go, at least I have no objections."

The phone began to ring in the office, and Park turned and went back in to answer it.

"What's your thought, Dr. George?" Carson asked.

"Several. We need a fast staff meeting to share options among ourselves, and then there are a bunch of facts that I think we can get at the Werner-Bok faster than the police can think to ask about them. I would like to get ahead of their investigation if possible. Quickly."

Park appeared in the door and came out looking closely at George as he approached.

"That was Fredericksburg. They've run the check on the Steele woman's roommate, and they've come up with a name."

He was watching George with an unaccountable, unblinking stare.

"Yes?" George asked.

"It seems the woman she lived with at U.Va. was called Grace Fairchild."

"Oh, Jesus," Carson said, and covered his eyes.

Chapter 19

CRIGHTON took one last look back toward where the men were standing. No one seemed to be looking in her direction, and she slid past the far side of the mansion and hurried toward the porch where the guide and the current crop of tourists could be expected to appear. She found she was already too late. The gardens were filled with visitors in twos and threes wandering around the geometrical paths. No sign of the guide.

She crossed the front of the house and went up the steps to the porch to get a higher view of the scene. There she located the woman at the extreme edge, standing alone just above the drop-off to the river. She seemed to be fixed, going nowhere. Crighton hurried down the steps and out the center path between the acrid-smelling boxwoods. She reached the far side of the formal gardens and crossed the lawn. The woman had not moved.

"Hello, may I interrupt you? I need to talk to you about something," Crighton said.

The guide turned as if both surprised by her presence and rather lost to reality. Crighton's question seemed to force her to return to the present. "Of course. How can I help?"

Crighton found the discussion on the lip of the bluff uncomfortable, and it occurred to her it might be wise to immobilize the woman for a second so she didn't rush off at the first word. She stepped back a few paces and said, "Could we sit down a moment? All this rushing back and forth is getting to me."

She dropped to the grass to show what she had in mind. The guide, wearing the rather tight skirt, hesitated for a second and then joined her, pulling her ankles under her.

"What's up?" she said.

"My name is Crighton Jones and I'm the information officer for the Werner-Bok Library in Washington," she began.

"Are you really? Very impressive place. I've used your manuscripts for research."

"Great—but not now. Something awful has happened and I don't want it to explode in your face. Things are always breaking out at the library and I'd give anything to have had a chance to collect my thoughts before I'm expected to deal with them. The point is, my friends and I were just up by your office and . . . there is no way to ease into this. A body has been found under the floor of that building you're in."

The guide did not shift her eyes from Crighton's and asked, "Do you mean an old, dead body? A historic body?"

"No. A person very recently murdered. I happen to know who it was, since the person was hoping to use one of our scholar rentals, and I had offered to put her up until she could find a room. It was a student from the University of Virginia. A Miss Durance Steele. She was —"

Crighton stopped, baffled by the way the guide was responding. The woman seemed completely frozen. She did not look away nor did she react, she simply kept on looking like she had before Crighton spoke. Then, ramrod straight, she raised her hands to her head and ran her fingers through her hair. At last she looked down at the ground and seemed to wipe sweat from her lips and chin. Crighton hesitated a moment to give her a chance to adjust and then the woman began to talk before Crighton could continue her report.

"Where was she?" the guide asked.

"Under the floor, right under one of the desks."

"Did someone tear up the floorboards?"

"No. There's an old door there—a trap door, or something."

"Who found her?"

"There's a state policeman there, and Elliott Brent led us all to it."

For the first time, there was a change of emotion. The guide smiled slightly, and said, "Elliott Brent. Isn't that interesting. Did he say how he knew it was there?"

"No, he acted like it was a surprise to him."

"Did he indeed." She smiled again, and then wiped her upper lip. "Miss Jones, I'm afraid I have something to tell you, too." She sighed and looked down at the lawn.

"My name is Grace Fairchild, and I was the roommate of that woman they've found—back at U.Va."

Crighton almost gagged with a sudden wave of nausea. "Oh, no! You hated her! You were hunting her like an—"

Fairchild looked surprised. "How did you know that?"

"The phone call and the card. They came to my apartment."

"Oh, I am sorry. They were meant for her."

"How did you get the number and the address?"

"She and I are . . . were involved in a bitter argument over some scholarly things and she had left word with the committee about where she could be reached. I got them to tell me. I thought it was a room she'd rented."

The full impact of the affair was beginning to hit

Crighton, and she found herself both bewildered and horrified.

"But you said you were going to kill her! Did you?"

Fairchild was getting herself under control faster than Crighton, and she smiled grimly. "I will tell you frankly there were many times I have wished I could, and I always wanted her to think I was going to, but I don't know what I really would have done if I'd had the chance. But no, I did not kill her. I never even saw her, dammit.

"Wednesday night when I closed up here, I saw her car in the parking lot. I recognized it immediately. We'd bought it together and we'd used it together for months. I looked all over the place for her, but I couldn't find her. I assumed she had gone right to the Brents and was working on them, but I could never catch up with her."

"You expected her?"

"Of course. I've been expecting her for a year. That's why I'm here. I came on some information in my research that would be embarrassing to people, and I agonized over whether I should reveal it or not. I finally decided I wouldn't. To my horror I found that Durr had copied my notes and *she* was going to use it herself. I tried to stop her—that's what the huge argument was about—but I found I was losing everywhere, so I used some family pull and got myself assigned here to protect the people . . . and things. I've been expecting her for months. Wednesday she came, but I never saw her."

"What would she have come for?"

"Extortion. She knew the family had lots of money and she thought she had a way to make them pay her to keep quiet."

"Had you warned them that she would try?"

"No. That wasn't appropriate."

"Do the Brents know about . . . about your role here?"

"No. In no way."

"If you didn't kill her, who did?"

"I'd rather not say," Fairchild replied, not unkindly, but sounding like it was not something to discuss with a stranger.

"How was she killed?" Fairchild asked.

Crighton wondered if she really did not know or if this was a ploy to establish her innocence. She was glad she could honestly say, "They don't know yet. They won't touch anything until the proper people arrive."

Fairchild sighed and said, "I guess I'd better face up to going back." She moved, but did not rise.

Crighton said, "The nephew has suggested that he saw you Wednesday in the middle of the night. Could he have?"

She took a deep breath and said, "Yes. After I spotted her car I went all over the grounds looking for her till it was dark, and then I went back to the office and faked a phone call to the big house. Martha answered and volunteered that she and Sarah were watching television. They sounded completely blah—nothing special going on, so I concluded that Durr wasn't inside. I waited till all the lights were out and everyone seemed to be asleep and then I did a careful search of everything—even down on the river—but there was no sign of her anywhere. I finally came back and went home. It must have been between two or three o'clock."

"He was saying something like 'the middle of the night.'"

Fairchild nodded without further comment.

Crighton asked, "The car was moved while we were with you."

Fairchild smiled slightly, and said. "Thanks for the alibi. I may need it."

"Do you know who moved it?"

"No," Fairchild said, but Crighton sensed she again had her suspicions about someone but felt it inappropriate to answer.

Fairchild put her palms on the grass, pushed herself to her knees, and then rose, dusting off her skirt and adjusting her uniform.

"Do I look properly authoritarian?" she asked sarcastically. "Or is that authoritative . . . or what? Anyway, it's time I faced the music."

Crighton rose with her and found herself swept with opposing emotions. If this was the woman of the phone call, she was despicable and deserved the worst the community could throw at her. But if this was the woman she had seen with her own eyes, she deserved her sympathy and support. She felt driven to express this dilemma aloud.

"Grace Fairchild," she said. "I hope you've been telling me the truth. If you have, I want to be on your side."

"I know you do," Fairchild said. "Thanks." She offered no further assurance and walked off toward her office alone, leaving Crighton staring after her. "'Betwixt I dare not and I would, like the poor cat i' the adage,'" Crighton recalled sourly. Was that Hamlet or P. G. Wodehouse? she wondered. Probably both, she concluded grimly, and followed slowly after the guide.

Chapter 20

"**M**URDER," Crighton said.

"Is that an expletive or a statement?" Carson asked.

"Both, dammit."

It was an hour later, and the three were sitting in an overlook off the George Washington Memorial Parkway, surrounded by the paper and plastic debris of a simple hamburger, fries, and milkshake. The detritus covered both seats of the car, and George wondered how so little fast food could require so much packaging for such a small amount of nutrition.

The final hour at the Belvoir Mansion had been without surprises. Park had been left in charge of the investigation, but the scene-of-the-crime crew had indeed relished the challenge, and had measured, photographed, interviewed, and recorded with vigor and apparent professionalism. Other than concluding that the woman had been killed by a blow from behind by a hard, edged instrument (that particular specialist had guessed either a hammer or the back of a hatchet), and that the death had occurred at least forty-eight hours before, little new had been established. Park assigned one of the patrolmen to concentrate on how the car had been moved to the airport, and as the three had left for Washington, Park and Fairchild were headed toward the Mansion to report the situation to the sisters Brent. George had felt great sympathy for the officer. He looked like he would rather have been almost anyplace in North America than on Lord Fairfax's plantation.

Crighton said bitterly, "I wish to God I knew whether I've been conned by some cynical, bloody bitch, or if I've hung a noose around the neck of a perfectly innocent, much put-upon victim." She stared across the Potomac below them with agony in her eyes.

"I can't reassure you, Crighton," George said. "Your concern is absolutely appropriate. And we all share your guilt. By telling Lieutenant Conrad about the threats, we all but wrote them a case against the Fairchild woman even before the crime was committed. But let's not waste time—or energy—on what we can do about it. She may indeed have done just what we've framed her with. What is essential now is that we find out quickly and accurately where truth lies—then we can either serve justice or undo the damage we've done."

"I'm with you but for a different reason," Carson said. "I think that prick of a nephew did it, and the quicker we nail him the better for all concerned. How do we start?"

"Very well," George said. "Let's check our unknowns—and join me with your own thoughts as we go along. First, there are those cursed books. They seem to have caused all the trouble. Are they real or is this all chaos over a might-have-been? Do we know what the books actually were before they were either burned or moved?"

"We know almost to the title," Carson answered. "The complete catalog was published as a pamphlet in 1812 and given to every congressman. We've got copies of it.

There's one on the table in Crighton's office. Presumably they bought more books in 1813 and 1814, but we at least know nine hundred titles from 1812."

"Only nine hundred? I thought—"

"Nine hundred titles, three thousand volumes. Print was larger and paper thicker in those days. Multi sets were very common."

"Understood. Then I'm going to call some rare book dealers and see if any of those nine hundred have come on the market since the Brents decided to give the house away. Maybe the combination of Madame Steele's extortion and the coming transfer of the property panicked somebody."

"Excellent. Can I join you?" Carson said.

"My pleasure. Next, I'd like to know what the people at the mansion think of Elliott Brent. What has he been up to, and what role does he play among the family?"

"Lovely. Anything that fries that little—"

"No, no," Crighton broke in. "Don't waste your time on that pipsqueak. So far as I'm concerned, what we've got to know is what's going on with Grace Fairchild. She's the key to this thing. What would you think if I talked to her alone? Is there anything wrong with that?"

"Providing you do it in a public place, I don't see why it wouldn't be very useful," George said.

"Would having dinner with her be appropriate? Eating somewhere—and women only, so I can watch her eyes."

"No reason for not. Just let us know where and when. Maybe Steve could deliver you and pick you up. Remember: if Fairchild killed the woman, you are her greatest threat. You're the one who could testify about the calls, maybe identify her voice, confirm the case we've spread all over officialdom. Don't ever be really alone with her. And speaking of how to preserve your future," George said casually, "what's the situation with you and the Werner-Bok these days? I'm liable to run into Nelson

Brooks one way or the other. Is there anything you want asked or any thoughts you want planted? How goes the career?"

"Oh, God," Crighton sighed, "one crisis at a time. I'm in a real mess with myself there. Don't tell Carson here, but I'm almost thirty and all the magazines say by thirty you're supposed to be on a path that will lead somewhere. My path leads between the desk and the wastebasket. Everybody treats me like they've got no complaints, and I suppose so long as I put in eight hours I can have the same job for thirty more years, but there's not another job in the building I can ever go to. And if I'm going to go anywhere else I've got to do it pretty quick or it's too late."

Carson said, "Why? Does someone say there's an occupational clock like the biological one? You know I'd love to help you with the latter, but I can't do much for your job."

"Don't be crude. I—"

"No, what do you want to be when you grow up?" Carson pursued.

"Don't fight me, you two. I'm not up to it today. You've put your finger right on the problem. I don't *know* what I want to be and everybody tells me I've got to hurry hurry hurry and make up my mind. Any moment now everything is going to turn into a pumpkin and . . ." Her voice was losing its timbre.

"Break!" Carson shouted. "Later—"

"Yes, yes," George said. "This isn't the time or the place. I should never have brought it up. Please, please forgive me. Let's face one thing at a time. And the one thing is, we've got to find out what happened and why before Brother Park and his friends try to tell *us*. I want to stay ahead of them. Let's move out, Steve. Maybe if we get more data, the connections will take care of themselves."

Carson started the car and got it onto the Parkway headed for Washington, quickly rising to the precise speed limit plus five.

"Forgive my unusually conservative driving," he said, "but this is not the time to attract the authorities."

Driving left-handed, he waved his other hand in the air and shouted, "A parable! A parable! Let me tell you two a parable. You made the mistake of saying 'connections,' Dr. George. You touch upon a delicate point. When I was on the second year of my masters, I got a Baby Fulbright for a semester in Europe, and I spent most of the time at the dig at Herculaneum. As you know, it's much richer than Pompeii and still barely a tenth dug out—but while I was there they were working on a cleaner's shop. Like everything else where they've excavated, it is precisely the way it was left in A.D. 80 or whenever the lava flowed over it—stuff on tables, food in pots, soaps and dyes exactly in place. Incredible. But up against a wall there was a perfectly preserved, *wooden* clothes press. It has a huge, vertical, wooden screw that pressed down on folded clothes, and the square board at the bottom is the exact size and shape of a folio book page.

"There is a wooden table right beside it, which is still perfectly preserved, and lying on it are bunch of little brass seals with the names of the customers on them. The names are in raised letters and they were used like rubber stamps at the post office. As God is my witness, there those things are, not two feet apart, but it took fourteen hundred years for Gutenberg to make the connection between a screw press and movable metal type! It absolutely paralyzed me when I saw it there, and it still stuns me today. I hope to God we can make the proper connections when *we* see 'em."

George beamed. "That's marvelous! I love it! You have set the challenge. On to the Werner-Bok!"

145

Chapter 21

T HE three had barely gotten through the bronze doors into the Great Hall when the opposition charged. The two strangers had apparently been casually walking across the marble space when they spied Crighton and did an abrupt pivot, bearing down on her like twin patrol boats in a television drug bust.

"Miss Jones! You're just the person we want to see!"

The thin man fixed her with an intent look, while an extremely heavy-set woman blocked any chance of moving on. George grinned at the action, recalling an old *Reader's Digest* joke: Why did you hit that fat lady, surely you could see her? Sure I saw her, I just didn't have enough gas to go around.

"Yes," the lady said, "what's going on about that Gutenberg?" The implication was that it was Crighton's fault.

Everyone came to a full stop and Crighton said, "Wait a minute, please. I don't know what you're talking about. Are you on the staff?"

"You know us. We're in the Law section, and they say

the library is going to buy a Gutenberg Bible for an outrageous sum of money."

"But we already have a Gutenberg."

"Don't we know it. That's why it's so asinine to spend that kind of money—money that the rest of us could use on something that really matters."

"How much money is this supposed to be?"

"Twelve million."

"You've got to be kidding."

"I know you're not supposed to discuss it, but it's disgusting to do this behind everybody's back until it's too late for anyone to do anything about it."

"I'm sorry, but I really have heard nothing about any of this. Let me look into it, and if there's anything that's appropriate to talk about, I promise you either I or someone will get back to you."

They clearly rejected this as a bureaucratic con, but could think of no other approach for the moment and said, somewhat on top of each other, "We'll call you. The staff has a right to know."

They grudgingly yielded the space, and Crighton headed for the elevator with Carson and George trailing respectfully behind like ministers following the queen.

As soon as the elevator door closed, Carson burst into a wide grin and said, "By God, it's great to know the real brass in a place as impressive as this."

"I haven't the slightest idea what they're talking about. Everybody thinks that the Public Relations Office is privy to every underhanded thing the library's up to so we can lie for Mahogany Row. The media mouthpiece, I guess. How would a rumor like that get started? Why would we want *two* Gutenbergs?"

George smiled and said, "The Folger has eighty First Folio Shakespeares."

"It does? Are they identical?"

"Very nearly."

"What does one of those cost?"

"The last one Yale bid on went for something over six hundred thousand dollars. I note ruefully that the experts we'd hired thought it'd go for four hundred thousand so our bid never even made it to the second round."

"Do you suppose there's anything to this Gutenberg thing?" Crighton asked with somewhat less assurance.

"It's possible, if you've got a pipeline to that kind of money. Gutenbergs come on the market every so often—there are still a few privately owned, and occasionally even an institution will unload one to build a new building or something. The University of Texas got a copy for two or three million a few years back."

"But two?"

"Oh, yes. If you could afford it, it'd be a great coup. Like a football team. Nobody'd heard of Leland Stanford until they bought a football team and then everybody said, 'Wow! If their football team is good enough to beat USC, they must be a real university'—and respect for their Ph.D.s promptly doubled. If you had two Gutenbergs, people would say, 'Wow! If their collection is so rich it has extra Gutenbergs just lying around, think what the rest of their holdings must be!' Could bring you in many times its cost in grants and endowments—not to mention visiting scholars."

"Would you do something like that in your own library?"

"I wouldn't touch it with a ten-foot pole. It would be an outrageous use of somebody else's money. I was just pointing out the case for the literary fringe."

"Did you say literary or lunatic?"

"As you wish."

"You're getting as hard to live with as Carson! I don't know how I got stuck with you two."

She led the way into her office smiling more cheerfully than she had all day.

They distributed themselves on various chairs and tables and George said, "All right, where's the list of the 1812 Library of Congress? I'd like to find out what we've got here. What's in it? What would it be worth to somebody if they actually had it in their cellar?"

Carson pulled a modern-bound little volume out of his stacked materials and handed it across. "This is a modern facsimile with an attractive introduction by the editor of the Madison papers. He's at the University of Virginia."

"Why do we keep banging up against U.Va. on this thing?"

"Coincidence."

"Oh."

"You're going to see what the original books are worth today?" Crighton asked.

"Right. Or to say it a different way, how rare are the things? Rare enough to kill somebody over?" George replied.

"Are there catalogs that give prices, or something?"

"For materials as old and as valuable as I suspect these are, we'll have to check auction records, because I suspect many of these titles would only come up once in a decade. For that we'll need *American Book Prices Current*. There should be a set in your reference room. We'll go look. While you always make life more interesting, Miss Crighton, if you need to catch up on your phone calls, Steve and I can work on this for a bit."

Crighton reluctantly accepted his offer, and ten minutes later the men were seated in a reading room with the facsimile in front of them and two red volumes of recent auction records on either side.

"All right," George said. "I'll take last year's, you do two years back. They're alphabetical by author and I see this 1812 catalog is arranged by subject, so it'll be clumsy, but let's start down the 1812 thing and see if any of them have come on the market in the past two years."

They drew blanks on the first four titles, but a current hit on the fifth.

"Appian's *History of the Punick, Parthian, and Civil Wars of the Romans*. London, printed 1679," George read quietly. "Folio size, one hundred sixty dollars."

"What do you mean, one hundred sixty dollars? Is that all it brought at the auction? For a book from 1679 half as big as a card table?"

"Hmmm. So it would seem. Let's move on."

A hit on the next volume.

"Another huge folio," George read. "Machiavelli's *Florentine History*. London, 1595. New York auction. Three hundred fifty dollars."

"Wait a minute—three hundred fifty dollars for a humongous book that's four hundred years old? That doesn't make sense."

"Hmm," George said. "Let's skip around and try some titles we recognize. Here's a first edition of Thomas Jefferson's *Notes on the State of Virginia*. Swann Galleries, last year, five hundred dollars. Here's Adam Smith's *Inquiry into the Nature and Causes of the Wealth of Nations*. London, 1796. Auctioned for sixty pounds. Let's try Malthus on the *Principle of Population*. Two volumes, 1806."

"I've got that one," Carson said. "It brought one hundred fifty pounds last year—in London. That's over two hundred dollars but still no staggering deal. I can't believe these figures. Are you sure we're understanding them right?"

"I think so, but maybe we'd better talk with the acquisition people. Go ask that librarian where they're located. I'll put these books back."

In another ten minutes they had gotten themselves to the Processing Department, and George was giving a laundered and condensed version of their situation to a strikingly stylish woman who looked like she might be a dramatics professor at a fashionable girls' school.

"So we kept coming up with these rather trivial prices, Mrs. Duncan. Does a fifty-dollar sale in *ABPC* really mean it sold for only fifty dollars?"

"Yes, that's what it means. Let me see the list."

George handed over the 1812 catalog and the woman fanned the pages quickly.

"Did you work all the way through it?"

"No, we started at the front and panicked after two or three pages."

"Then that's your trouble. A rare book is only worth what someone is willing to pay for it. You may have the world's only copy of a book about Icelandic Gypsies, but until you find somebody interested in Iceland or Gypsies, it isn't worth a penny. Your trouble was you were looking in the social sciences—history and government. Social scientists are either very niggardly or don't have time to read old books. That area of rare books is notoriously cheap. Let's look at geography or the hard sciences. Follow me, please."

They went to the end of the room where a wall was filled with catalogs and price records from floor to ceiling. She pulled a current copy of *American Book Prices Current* and motioned them to sit beside her.

"You read off the titles from the 1812 collection. I'll search the auction record. Start with the sciences."

George found the proper section and said, "Wilson's *American Ornithology*. Philadelphia, 1808."

Very quickly the librarian replied, "Two sold. One for four thousand dollars and one for three thousand five hundred dollars."

"What?" Carson said. "Let me see that."

He leaned over her arm, and said, "Yep, just like the ones we found. Try another."

"Diderot's *Encyclopedie*. Paris, 1751. One volume."

"Two copies sold last year. One for two thousand four hundred pounds and one for three thousand six hundred

151

pounds," Mrs. Duncan said with a slight note of "didn't I tell you?" in her voice.

"Amazing," George said.

"Let's do a few travel books," she said. "I think you'll be even more surprised."

George flipped to the section of the catalog titled "Geography and Topography, Voyages and Travels."

"Hawkesworth's *Account of the Voyages in the Southern Hemisphere*. London, 1773," he read.

"Two copies sold at auction last year. One for four thousand two hundred dollars and one for five thousand five hundred."

"Pike's *Expedition to the Sources of the Mississippi*. Philadelphia, 1810."

"Two copies auctioned. Both two thousand dollars."

"Philip's *Voyage to Botany Bay*. 1790."

"Here's a 1789 edition sold for three thousand two hundred pounds. No mention of a 1790."

"Well," George closed the facsimile and leaned back. "You have certainly made your point and we are much in your debt. Apparently there are at least one hundred fifty or two hundred geography books here. There are that many more science things, plus whatever the remainder of the collection might bring, which could easily add up to half a million dollars."

"How many books total?"

"Nine hundred titles, three thousand volumes."

"Then your estimate would certainly seem valid. I would have said half to three-quarters of a million. I noticed a few things that we've bought ourselves, and they were all in multiple thousands of dollars. Incidentally, I think I saw three copies of *The Federalist* on your list, and it's selling for in excess of three thousand dollars for the 1788 edition—which those were. There are a few expensive ones even among the social sciences."

"Well, this has been extraordinarily helpful. You have

152

advanced our puzzle enormously. Tell me, please—and we certainly don't expect you to do it for us—but is there any way to know who sold the copies we've found here? We're working on a single collection of books that have belonged to a single Southern family, and we are wondering if they are selling them off either one at a time or possibly en bloc. There was that bird book, for example."

"Wilson."

"Yes. Is there any way of finding out if it came from our family?"

"Not from our records here—what you're asking is for the book's 'provenance'—but it is usually known by both the buyer and the seller. It's the way you protect yourself from buying a stolen volume that the real owner would have a perfect right to snatch back from you if he found it on your shelves, and it could be very difficult to recover your money. No, I think the best way for you to proceed is to take a few unusual volumes—ones that only appear for auction occasionally—and simply make some calls. I must admit, I'm rather intrigued to know if my solution would actually work. Would you object to my trying it on a few titles, or would that cause difficulties?"

"Great heavens, no," George said. "That would be wonderful, but I certainly don't want—"

She held up her hand to cut him off. "Then let me have the book and I'll pick out a few targets. Is it appropriate to ask what family would be involved?"

"No problem. The name would be Brent, if they're not using an alias."

She looked down at the book in her hand, and looked up quizzically. "This is the lost Library of Congress collection. You're not suggesting that that family would have their own copies of all of these? What if I select a half-dozen titles and they aren't actually among the ones the Brents owned?"

"Oddly enough," George replied, "if the family had

any of those, it is probable they had *all* of those. I didn't go into it when we barged in on you, because I didn't want to use up that much of your time, but if you have three minutes, I'd love to provide a little more detail."

Five minutes, not three, later, he had brought Mrs. Duncan into the problem, and ten minutes later she was at her desk with her Rolodex of dealers in front of her and her phone in her hand.

Thirty minutes beyond that she leaned back in her chair and said, "As you must have gathered from what you heard at this end, I think we have established the following: I selected five sample titles, all very valuable. Three of the dealers had never seen any of them in their memory. Two had handled at least one of them in the past five years and they will call us back with the names of the people who put those up for sale. And the final two dealers had not *seen* any of the five titles but have had all five offered to them, for sale, within the past ten days. The potential seller was one Elliott Brent. He visited their offices in person and claims that if they can agree on a price, he can deliver the volumes within a week. The five sample titles I was using are among a list of nearly a hundred titles Brent had left with the two dealers."

"Ah," said George.

"Miracle Woman," said Carson. "It has been one of the prime experiences of my life to watch you work."

Chapter 22

"WHERE have you been?" Crighton greeted them as they entered her office. "All sorts of excitement. The director wants to have dinner with you. In his office. Seven o'clock. I'm set for same with Grace Fairchild half an hour earlier in Alexandria. And, oh yes," she smiled wickedly, "Lieutenant Park called. They're ready to make an arrest but they want to talk to you first."

"What!" Steve shouted. "Arrest who?"

"Apparently Elliott Brent, but he didn't spell it out. That only came out when he admitted that Elliott's disappeared. He's fit to be tied—Park, that is."

"You're making this up," Carson said. "Brent? We've just established that he spent the week in New York— and probably can prove he was there during all the possible times for the murder, too, dammit."

"Not necessarily, Steve," George said. "All we know is he was there from Friday to Wednesday—but only during working hours. As I've proved myself on too many occasions, you can work in New York up to five o'clock, grab the six o'clock shuttle to National, and be anywhere in

Washington by dark. Same thing in reverse going back up on the seven o'clock in the morning. The air time is only forty minutes. He could have spent any or all of his days in New York and been back at Belvoir for the night. It's only a twenty-minute taxi from National. What is Park basing his charges on, Crighton?"

"I have no idea. His call was to you and he claimed he had something to show you at Belvoir. He wants you to come right down. Do you want to go?"

"Let's see, it's three-thirty. We could be there in forty-five minutes. Let me call Brooks and tell him supper is fine, and then we'll go. Can you get away, Crighton?"

"Of course. Let me phone for you. What did you two learn about the books?"

George smiled. "Well, quite a lot of almosts. We almost know that the lost library actually exists. Brent is offering chunks of it to rare book dealers around New York, and while it's possible that he just *hopes* it's in the Belvoir cellar—and in fact he's working from the same list we are—it's not likely. Surely he's had his hands on the volumes he's peddling."

"Have you got a firm motive?"

"Just almost. The collection seems to be worth well over half a million dollars. If Steele was about to frustrate or even threaten the sale of those books, the loss of that much money might be enough to do her in. Added to that, she would probably have put the threat in as ugly a way as possible, so a mixture of fury and greed would 'almost' be enough to account for murder. But we must ask the other side of the question: does Elliott Brent have enough nerve to kill somebody with his bare hands?"

"I'd vote yes to that," Carson said. "Not because of guts but because of his contempt for mankind. We fellow beings are just a step above the asp in his eyes, not just below the angels. He could knock someone off without flickering an eye."

"While you're not the most objective judge in this case," George smiled, "I'm inclined to agree with you. All right, Crighton, if you can get me the director, we'll get started."

Crighton reached for the phone. "You know there actually is something going on about that Gutenberg thing. Incredible. Brooks has promised to brief me when we can agree on a time. Someone has actually offered them a second copy and the high levels are all excited. They're actually flying in a big name from England to help them decide. I couldn't believe it. Here's Mrs. Ferrar."

She handed the phone to George.

One hour later they were turning into the Belvoir Mansion drive.

Carson was saying, "That bookkeeper is too meek to be true. I got the feeling that he'd been pretty well beaten down by the Brents—friend Elliott in particular. He might be good for a little pumping. Does either of you object to my seeing what I can learn?"

"Fine by me," George said. "Go to it. And there's Park by that cruiser."

Carson angled the car over to where the officer was standing by a police car, talking into a hand-held transmitter. By the time they had parked, the lieutenant had signed off and returned the instrument to the dashboard. He walked toward them alone. There was no evidence of the guide, Grace Fairchild.

"Hello," he said. "Thanks for coming down. A few things have turned up and I wanted your reaction. What I mean is, in the light of what you know about the situation, do these things mean what I think they mean?"

"We'll be happy to guess with you," George said. "Where do you want us?"

"Out back. Or front. Or whatever the hell you call that garden by the river."

As they started off, Carson stopped and turned back toward the car. "Go ahead," he said. "I'll catch up with you."

The remaining three headed around the mansion, and the officer explained as they walked. "One of the things that seemed so odd was why, with all the strange places there are on this plantation, somebody would try to hide a body under that office floor where people are coming in and out all day. At first I thought it meant that the Fairchild woman had killed Steele by her own desk and hid her right there so she could keep track of her. Then we came on what I want to show you."

They walked to the center of the formal garden with its trimmed aisles of boxwood and then passed off to the right toward a long space that paralleled the river. Here the beds were filled with great mixes of flowers, like informal English cottage gardens.

"The bookkeeper says that this area was originally where they raised vegetables for the big house. It grew what the people ate during the summer. Now it pretty much belongs to the two Brent women, and they plant flowers from seed every year."

"Annuals," Crighton said.

"Right. Well, you see that mound of stuff on the far side there? That's a compost pile. Apparently the two women spend as much time fussing with that as they do on the flowers themselves—they mix chemicals and stuff in with the leaves and grass, and it's been there for years."

By now they had reached the site and the officer had stopped beside an empty circular area surrounded by a new, waist-high snow fence. The new area sat immediately beside a weather-beaten and similarly fenced compost pile almost chest high.

"According to the bookkeeper, the ladies had been planning a second one of these mulch things, and it had

158

been started in that circle. Now, look in the middle. Do you see how someone has dug a fresh hole six feet long and two feet wide? My guess is that whoever killed Steele expected to put her into that hole, put the dirt back, and spread some of the compost over her. And if they had, she could have laid there for years before anyone would have thought to look. With the body under the compost and the car gone, somebody must have thought no one would ever know anything. The point is, the spot under the floorboards was just a temporary way station till the body could be put inside that fence for good. Oh, by the way, we found the keys to the Porsche and the contents of the girl's handbag under some papers in the back of Fairchild's file cabinet."

"Ummm. Between Fairchild being seen by the river in the middle of the night, the body under her own floorboards, and the personal effects in her files, aren't you suggesting this seems to point to Fairchild?" George asked.

"Maybe. At least we're supposed to think so. Fairchild admits she was in her office till late on the night of the murder. But then we came on this mess about Elliott Brent."

The lieutenant started back toward the mansion, talking as he walked.

"I put a guy named Thompson on that sports car business, and he broke it so quickly I can't decide if the guy who did it was that clumsy, or wanted us to figure it out as quickly as we did.

"The car was so easy to spot that the airport police made it on the first pass. The ticket was inside on the dash and it was stamped eleven forty-two. You get the ticket out of a machine on the way in, so no one could identify who was driving the Porsche, but a driver of the very next Fort Belvoir bus—which leaves the airport at noon—remembers carrying an adult civilian male who stood out from the rest of the uniforms and the recruits with their suitcases. After you pass Mount Vernon there are three street stops and then the Belvoir Mansion gate, the Fort Belvoir dependents' housing shed, and finally the three stops at the Fort itself—"

"Is this a part of the Fort?"

"No, the Mansion property runs along the side and it's all fenced off separately. Belongs to the state. The Fort's federal. The point is, the noon bus driver remembers the civilian getting off at the mansion stop, and he's sure he could pick the guy out. It's got to be Brent."

George said, "We found out he was in New York trying to sell some of the family books, and he does seem to have witnesses for the daytime hours."

"Well, that's another of the weird things about Brent," Park said. "He bought the ticket for the return shuttle on the plane and with cash, so there was no credit card reference or name on a voucher, but then he wrote his real name on the sign-in sheet at La Guardia. No attempt to cover himself. Same thing about the Porsche at the airport. Unless there was someone using it we don't know about, it looks like he put it in the airport lot to make it look like she'd left town and she'd never been anywhere else. But he makes no attempt to cover his own trail, takes a public bus directly to Fort Belvoir, and simply goes home in broad daylight. Either he's up to something we don't know about yet, or he's incredibly stupid."

"It's one explanation," George said. "What does Brent say when you charge him with all this?"

Park looked down and then at George with a combination of embarrassment and anger. "We haven't seen him since shortly after you left."

"Had you told him to stay on the premises?"

"Yes, and without his knowledge we've got a plain car parked across from the entrance. He didn't go that way, but there are all sorts of trails through the woods and the shortest cut to the Fort bus stop is a footpath off through the bushes there. You can get a cab at the Fort, too."

"You can also walk along the river, I think."

Park looked like he hadn't thought of that, and it further distressed him.

"We'll get him, but we look a little foolish."

"Did you search the mansion?"

"Sort of. We did a visual of all the floors, but the women were getting stuffier all the time, and I thought we'd save the tear-up-the-place till we were sure there wasn't some easier explanation."

"So you think it's Brent."

"I do. Miss Jones here told Conrad that the Steele woman was after some books. Brent was trying to sell some books. Brent planted the body in here with Fairchild to implicate her. Brent led us to the body. Brent moved the car to confuse things. Brent put the driver's license and the keys to the Porsche in the back of Fairchild's files. He thinks he's framed the guide. I think he's got one big surprise coming."

Had Carson been there, he would have agreed with the lieutenant, but Carson was in the guide's office looking for hard facts and firm proof. He had headed straight for the bookkeeper the moment the other three had disappeared from sight, and was pleased to find him in precisely the same spot he had occupied before. He was still keying the calculator, and he was still surrounded by open ledgers. This time, he seemed to be writing checks as well.

"Hi!" Carson said. "I seem to have missed my friends. Where's the guide here? Can I wait in her chair?"

"She's giving a tour. Do whatever you want."

Carson dropped into place and looked back at the other man. He was in his forties, thin, with straight gray hair that he had greased into place. Carson thought, he looks like one of fifty people coming out of a subway exit in a

161

black-and-white movie. A plastic deskplate said NORMAN PHELPS.

"Are you from around here?" Carson asked.

"No. California."

"California! What are you doing back here?"

"That's what everyone asks. Why is it if you're in California and say you're from Virginia, everybody says, oh. But if it's backward, it's a big deal? Real California arrogance, and everybody buys it."

Carson laughed. "I guess that's true. Do you have any Virginia ties? Pre-California kin?"

"No. My father was a lawyer with Western Pacific and when its president, Burton Herrington, set up his library and art gallery in Marin County my father got me a job as their fiscal officer. I was there for twenty years. Then when Getty did his art gallery, the Herrington heirs lost all interest in the library side and shut it down and I was redundant. Fortunately, Western Pacific had been bought by Norfolk and Richmond, which is controlled by the Brents, and I was able to slip across the organization. They thought what I did there sounded like what they needed to be done here, so I've been here for the past three years."

"Working with their books, you mean?"

"Oh, no. Closing down their house and land—like we closed down the Herrington holdings. As you can see, I keep getting jobs that do away with any place for me to work."

"Can't you go over to the state when Belvoir is passed over?"

"No. The state is civil service. I couldn't get in for years."

"Sorry. Bum deal. Have you enjoyed working here?"

"No. At first it was fine—keeping their records, doing their taxes, and working on their investments. But they treat me like a yard man. I don't ask to be treated as their

162

equal, but I do ask to be treated like a professional. I finished all the requirements for a C.P.A. I'm not a clerk, but they don't seem to know it."

"Who do you deal with mostly?"

"Mostly the women. I try to avoid the nephew as much as possible."

"What will happen to the nephew when the mansion goes?"

"God only knows. Not only is he totally incompetent, no one could stand to have him around."

"Is he handicapped or something?"

"Oh, no. Only by his money and his name. He thinks he can walk on water and he's never found anyone worth associating with."

"Where do you live around here?"

"Over toward Orange—across from Madison's house. Montpelier. It was owned by the Du Ponts and they gave it to the National Trust. It's a good location for me. It's about equidistant between Charlottesville and here. I come this way during the week and go to U.Va. on weekends."

"Are you taking courses?"

"No, no. Just using their research materials."

"On what?"

"Western trails. When I was a kid I traced the whole Oregon Trail during three summers in a beat-up Chevrolet. Then after college, I did the Santa Fe Trail, and then when I was at the Herrington, I got interested in Lewis and Clark. Jeez, there was real adventure."

"Why would U.Va. have *western* trail materials?"

"Meriwether Lewis, of course. And Jefferson. Lewis lived in Charlottesville and the family is still there."

"Oops. Never thought of that. Did Jefferson ever get west?"

"No, he dreamt of it—he conceived of the expedition way back in 1785 when he was minister to France—but he never got farther west than Staunton, Virginia, himself. Never got farther south than North Carolina—some people think he never went that far—that he never left Virginia going south. But he could dream. God, that expedition was something. There's never been anything like it since. Twenty-nine men, six thousand miles, and they only lost a single person—from appendicitis. Indians, blizzards, trackless mountains. Marvelous experience."

"The Brents were in the house then?"

"Oh, yes, they'd been here for twenty-five years by 1804. Lots of the explorers came from around here, but nobody came from this plantation. They've always been too busy making money and taking no chances. You'd never see a Brent getting mixed up with anything like that."

Carson smiled. "I detect a slight lack of loyalty to the lord and master."

"They've never shown any loyalty to me and I keep making them richer." He tapped the ledger that was under his right hand, and then went silent.

Carson thought it was time to take his leave, and did.

Chapter 23

SIX-THIRTY Friday evening. George had been returned to the library, and Steve and Crighton had doubled back to Alexandria. Steve stopped the car beside a pub sign, which was hanging into a tiny, darkened alley that ran between decayed brick walls.

"'The Wanderer,'" he read. "Well, that's supposed to be it, but it looks like something out of a *Treasure Island* set. Bristol and drunken pirates shouting for rum."

"Grace Fairchild said it was a 'nice place' and 'kind of interesting.'"

"And the door is down that alley?"

"So it appears."

"Hmmm," he said uncertainly.

"I'll be fine. Where'll you be when I need to be collected?"

Carson looked up and down the street and spotted a fireplug midblock on the opposite curb. "I'll pull into that space by the plug and just sit there from seven-thirty on. If I get as bugged as I suspect I will, I'll be back in fifteen minutes and start waiting. Don't worry about me. Somebody once said there's an average of thirty-five restaurants per block in Old Town Alexandria, so there'll be plenty to look at."

"Knowing what you'll be staring at, you're more likely to be roughed up than I am. Okay, I'm off. I must admit, I'm a little less casual about this than is my usual wont." She exhaled a large breath and resolutely turned to go down the narrow passage.

Halfway down the right-hand building there was a blackened door set back in the wall with the words THE WANDERER incised in a brass plaque. She pushed her way in and found herself in a beautifully restored pub with a small fire burning discreetly in an open fireplace opposite a huge, time-darkened bar.

"Have you a table for a Miss Fairchild?" she asked the collegian carrying the menus.

"Miss Fairchild is here. Follow me, please."

Grace Fairchild was waiting in a soft, stylishly designed dress, and Crighton realized that she had never seen her in anything but a gabardine twill uniform. God, Crighton thought, Carson would have melted into a damp puddle if he'd been here.

They exchanged salutations as Crighton sat down in the high-backed booth. There was barely enough light to read the selections by, but the polished brass fittings sparkled against the shadows.

"I thought you might enjoy this. It was a Civil War stable, believe it or not, and these were stalls before the tables and benches were put in. If you keep walking, you come on a splendid formal dining room complete with white linen and hurricane glasses on the candles, but it's easier to talk here."

"Wow, this does look genuine. And it really is? Worn brick floors and all?"

"Alexandria is a strange blend of colonial, with the Washingtons and Lees and Mason homes still standing all

166

around, and Civil War, with the Lees and Fitzhughs and Armistead houses standing right beside them. Poverty did it. The town fell into a monumental depression after the war and nobody had any money to tear down and build bigger and better and newer. It left quite a treasure house of eighteenth- and nineteenth-century architecture."

"Are the old families here, too—like you said about the Tidewater?"

"Oh, heavens, yes. There are some blocks in Alexandria that have the same names on the mailboxes they did in antebellum times."

"What happened to the people at Belvoir?"

"The Fairfaxes or the Brents?"

"I meant the Fairfaxes—Lord Fairfax, was it? Did they all go back to England?"

"Just Sally and George William, Washington's friends—and remember, they were the cousins who ran the family holdings. The Lord Fairfax himself—Baron Cameron—was Thomas, and he blithely gave up the title after the Revolution, moved to a farm in the Shenandoah Valley, and lived to his nineties as plain Tom Fairfax. He was gay, by the way, and he lived with six or eight male friends who were much loved by their neighbors in Winchester."

Fairchild laughed. "The Fairfaxes had been breeding like rabbits up to the Revolution, so they were scattered all over Virginia, and everybody stayed here. The pastor of Christ Church here in Alexandria was a Fairfax for the early part of the 1800s, several of the children went into politics, and one of the local sons did the whole Gold Rush bit in '49 and ended up as one of the first speakers of the California Assembly and the clerk of the California Supreme Court. Would you believe it? He married and settled in Marin County in the 1850s. The Fairfaxes knew good real estate wherever they found it."

They ordered and began to eat, talking of trivial matters until Crighton remembered Carson presumably sitting in the dark, and she took a deep breath and brought matters to a focus.

"Your own work was always the colonial period, I presume."

"The graduate work, yes," Fairchild answered. "All the troubles that led me to this booth," she smiled grimly, "started when I was thrashing around for a thesis topic.

"I was first impressed with the way that both the upper and the working classes of the 1750s thought they were living in the best of all possible worlds. 'An Augustan age,' the planters kept calling it, and you could see how they came by the impression. There had been no major war for decades. Everybody had a job. Everybody was reasonably well housed. There was an astonishing amount of culture and books and music and even the social services coming out of the parish system took remarkable care of everybody. Remember, at the time of Williamsburg and Belvoir there was an enormous amount of money flowing around. The great homes—Westover, Carter's Grove— were often paid for by the profits of a single year's tobacco crop. There was law and justice. The only horrible flaw was the unthinkable one of human slavery.

"So I started to ask how could this have been tolerated by such decent people as Washington and the Lees and the Jeffersons—and that got me more confused than ever, because I discovered that the picture was terribly mixed. Less than half of the Virginia families had any slaves at all, and by the turn of the century most of the names we know had freed theirs—Washington and Wythe and many of the Lees. By 1820 there were as many free blacks right here in Alexandria as there were slaves, and more blacks owned property than whites did. But Thomas Jefferson hadn't released his, yet he was more sensitive to individual freedom than anybody.

"So I started down that path trying to find out what the

Jefferson story was—as you know, at U.Va. Mr. Jefferson is so real you expect to meet him at the end of his curving walls—and I found the answer: he couldn't afford to. Most of his slaves were actually chattels that were security to somebody else and he couldn't free them, and even if he could, once freed he'd have to pay them wages so they could live and he had no money at all. Everything was in hock to somebody. He didn't even dare let them leave Monticello—he had to keep it producing to keep it from being seized and broken up by the creditors and the slave families broken up and sold off a person at a time.

"And then I backed into how the debts were paid. He sold furniture and distant farms and canal shares and finally those damn books—twenty-four thousand dollars worth. And from the books, I got into the burning—"

"Wait a minute, before you get to that," Crighton interrupted, "would you explain something about that. Why didn't he just declare bankruptcy and start over? From what little I know from television biographies, practically everybody who was anybody went bankrupt at least once. General Grant and Mark Twain and half the presidents. Why did Jefferson make such a big deal of it?"

"It just 'wasn't done' among the Virginia aristocracy. It sounds odd, but there really was a code that they'd rather be dead than violate. Life really wouldn't have been worth living for them.

"It's a fascinating phenomenon. The children of the planters got the code astonishingly early . . . there was an image they were taught to fit, and they passed it down from one generation to the next, one family to the next. At the time of Belvoir, for example, the planters' kids got a conscious schooling in the management of affairs and the handling of people. From the very first they were made aware of their privileged status and they were taught the habit of command. They *expected* to rule. They were taught to reach decisions quickly—hell, they even walked like aristocrats. We have English visitors writing home about how the Virginians all carried themselves erect, were good horsemen, and were uniformly self-assured. Read arrogant?"

"Do you think there really is a sense of Southern noblesse oblige—honor?"

"It's tricky. Very subtle. The 'public man' was supposed to have 'simplicity'—the opposite of 'cleverness' or self-interest. He was supposed to maintain a public appearance for the sake of its honor, not the salary or the fringe benefits. You find it in all the seven Virginia presidents, and in political roles right down to the present. You didn't deserve to be a leader in the community unless you served selflessly on boards and commissions and God knows what. The sisters Brent are right in the tradition. They're very self-confident doers. They ride and hunt and garden and are acutely aware of the value of a dollar. The southern woman perceived herself as the keeper of the family flame. The land was her responsibility, the children, the patrimony. The aristocratic Virginia woman was never the delicate magnolia—or mousey spinster—that we read about in Spanish-moss country. They are expected to be self-assured and gutsy, no matter how feminine they may act."

"So what did you finally decide to do about the thesis?"

"Well, you know even while I try to convince myself I'm an independent, modern woman, I have to admit I've got the family's 'certain things aren't done' inside me, too. Although I try not to let it out, we're F.F.V. ourselves, you know—and I couldn't be the one that revealed that Jefferson's book money came by hiding the Library of Congress so his friends could claim they had to buy a new one. This has lain quietly for a hundred years; *I* couldn't be the one who turned on the light. So after a year of collecting notes, I abandoned the whole thing.

"I got involved with a man at about the same time and

went to live with him and this infuriated Durance Steele. I couldn't believe she could go from being the best friend I'd ever had to a savagely bitter enemy, but by the time I realized what had happened, she'd copied all the Jefferson material and was going to build a reputation on it. At first I was simply frantic. I tried to get the topic certified as prior research and she beat me on that. Then I threatened her with exposure and that I'd tell the profession that she'd stolen it all. I told her I'd see that she never got a degree. In desperation, I threatened to cut her up in her own blood. She wouldn't stop. It was all a way to get even with me for what she claimed I'd done, and with what she'd perceived as personal slights by 'my class,' as she called it. We both went more than a little crazy over it, and when I finally got myself under control I tried to get myself ahead of her and in a position to block her."

"Do you think Jefferson knew the collection had never been burned? That it was all a ruse to give him money?"

"No. He'd accumulated the books as an ambassador, cabinet officer, and president, and he'd always intended to give the collection to the nation somehow, but when he began to get desperate about his credit situation, he simply tried everything, and when he heard the Capitol had been burned, he offered the Monticello collection as a replacement. He simply moved up the time. I think his Democratic friends saw it as a chance to move some money to him and took over the idea. Remember, there was nothing like a presidential pension in those days, yet they expected an ex-president to keep playing the role. Jefferson entertained literally dozens of foreign visitors for weeks at a time at Monticello."

"You really think the three thousand books still exist, then?"

"Oh, yes."

"That's why you came to Belvoir? To protect the books?"

"What they represent—the family, the secret, everything."

"Do you think the books are at Belvoir now?"

"They were there. Probably still are."

"You haven't seen them?"

"No."

"Durance Steele believed all this, too?"

"Yes. She concentrated on it, and worked it out in far greater detail than I had."

"What was she going to do at Belvoir that day she got there?"

"Maybe look for the books, but more important, she would be demanding silence money. If you don't pay me, I'll tell. I'll tell about Jefferson and fraud and questionable use of public funds and how you Brents have hidden this deception for umteen generations. Oh, God . . ." Fairchild's voice seemed strangled.

"Did you know that Elliott Brent was starting to sell the volumes? Dr. George found at least two dealers in New York who'd been offered a mess of the most expensive ones."

"Oh, dear," Fairchild said. "The coming transfer of the house must have forced that. Durr's messing around would have screwed up the sale. If she'd known what he was up to, she'd have demanded to be cut in on the profits. If he'd refused, she'd wreck the sale for everyone by revealing the books really belong to the government."

"Could this have tripped Elliott into murdering her?"

Fairchild paused and then said flatly, "It's not for me to say."

Crighton said with irritation, "Look. I do want to believe you, but you must realize that you can take everything you've just said about Durance Steele and fit it around yourself. Even if you came to Belvoir for the best of reasons, once you saw what Steele was doing you knew that really the only way to stop her—to shut her mouth

172

forever—was to kill her. She was going to 'reveal all,' maybe even steal the books themselves. Murder was the only thing that would really work."

"I know."

"Well, can't you give me any assurance that that wasn't what happened? That you didn't do it? What can you give me to defend you with?"

"I don't know. I haven't been able to figure that out."

"Oh, come on! Forgive me, I'm trying to be as candid as I know how, but I have to tell you that I can think of an explanation that hangs on, What if you hadn't stopped her? What if this blew sky-high and you knew it would never have happened if you hadn't started the mess and it occurred because you never did what was necessary to stop it? What if you had to live the rest of your life with that thought? Have you ever thought that way?"

"Many times."

"And what was the answer?"

"I would have to kill her."

"As a high moral act?"

"No, as grim, satisfying, glorious release and resolution! Great, passionate, crystalline joy."

Thirty minutes later, when Crighton climbed into the car beside Carson, she said, "God damn it. Not only don't I know any more than I did when I started, now I don't even know which side I'm on."

"But the murder. . . ?"

"I think she did it. Maybe for all sorts of good reasons, but she did it."

She stared down the darkened street a moment, lit only by the soft gaslights, and then said, "Let's go home, please. I'm tired. I'm tired all over and I want to think."

173

Chapter 24

$\mathbb{A}$ FEW moments before seven o'clock, George had put down the books he had been studying in Crighton's office and started up to the director's sanctum. While the basement administrative offices were silent, with closed doors, the Great Hall had been quietly rumbling with continuing busloads of tourists swarming in and out to contemplate the rarities. The galleries around the Great Hall had been almost as busy with readers and researchers coming off elevators and going into the specialized reading rooms. Both hall and rooms would be open until ten o'clock, and each would serve more patrons after the dinner hour than during the previous eight. George was ready for his food. The seven o'clock appointment had matched his usual supper time, but the midafternoon hamburgers had not satisfied his usual requirements. He wondered where food would come from in a closed library at this time of night.

The door to the director's office was closed, but George pushed his way in and crossed the ornate waiting room, without the usual dignified supervision of Mrs. Ferrar. George tapped on the director's door and was shouted in.

"Come in, come in," Brooks yelled. He was struggling to his feet from behind the huge desk when George entered. "Good to see you! Delighted you could come. I should warn you right off that we're limited to cold plates and vichyssoise, but if you can take it, have a seat. Otherwise I'll follow you to the nearest bistro."

"That'll be splendid," George said as he sank into one of the leather chairs. He had surreptitiously spied a table set for two at the side, so he would be spared any knee-balancing act—a form of feeding that had repulsed him for over half a century.

"Well. Your morale any better?"

"No. Two of the things I was supposed to chair this afternoon got canceled, so I had time to brood on my frustrations. Never a good idea."

"I am increasingly convinced," said George, "that our problems are stemming from a flawed way we've viewed our job. As librarians, we thought we were book people. That people came to our buildings to get books. This was a mistake. It had no more validity than thinking people sit down before a television set to fiddle with knobs. The knobs only get the television working. The books were only the things that held the facts or images the people were after. Now that the book is evaporating before our eyes we think all is lost—"

"Is the book really evaporating," Brooks interrupted, "or does it just seem that way?"

"Oh, no. It is specifically getting fewer and fewer. Every year, fewer commercial titles are printed. Fewer new authors have to be established in the catalog. And even worse, every year there are fewer people who could read a book if there were books to read. Absolute illiteracy is up, but relative illiteracy is even worse. Just because we

175

can sweep-read a page, we assume everyone can. Not so. Ask your nephew with the new master's to read you a paragraph. Ten to one you'll be horrified to find he reads one word at a time, very deliberately."

"Yeah, I've had that happen too many times to make me happy, but there are lots of kids who still live in a world of books—read 'em by the yard like we used to."

"Your error is in your 'lots.' You should have said some. Book readers are getting to be like opera buffs. 'Everybody I know loves opera,' an opera nut will tell you, and it's true. It's just that everyone in their world ain't many because their world is really very small. An island among ordinary people. Every year there are fewer of us in the reading world. Everybody we know reads lots and buys more books than ever. But there ain't as many everybodys as there were ten years ago.

"But wait a minute. You interrupted me. My point was, that that isn't so bad. It's the facts and the images of imagination that really mattered, and people want them just as badly and use them just as much as ever. The old devices for allusions have slipped away because ordinary people use different images. You don't say the Count of Monte Cristo for revenge, you say Clint Eastwood, make my day! You don't use Shakespeare and the Bible and Dickens, you use sitcoms and comic strips and movies. Different images in fancy and—just as hard for us—different sources for facts. What people like you and me have got to give up is our annual reports and our statistical abstracts, and we've got to get used to asking the on-line nets instead. The numbers are the same, still needed, just kept in a different place."

Brooks laughed grimly. "I find when most of my scholars want a number they don't look anywhere! They sit down at a telephone and keep calling until they're finally referred to somebody who really does know."

"And you have to admit that that's a gain," George replied. "When they took it out of our books, it was by definition a year old via preparation, printing, proofing, binding, and whatever before it got on the shelf. The guy on the phone probably worked up his new figures only yesterday."

"So all we've got to do is keep stacks of optical disks with long lists of computer log-ons, and we're right back where Melvil Dewey started. Right?"

"Right. The only problem is, the one time we've tried something like that, we've lost heavily. I thought computerizing our catalogs would open up great vistas of new connections and delicate interrelationships. All we did was blind the old folks who knew what a catalog card was and reduce the computer kids to thinking our controls are a telephone directory. Ummm."

"Come on," Brooks said, "let's start the food. The cafeteria folks loaded my refrigerator. Let's see what we've got."

Together they covered the conference table at the side of the room with edibles, and started to work.

"So how's your project coming? Are you pleased with your progress?" Brooks asked.

"Fair question. I'm in one of those rare instances where I'm not sure I'm happy with what I've worked so hard to learn. Do you remember Mark Twain's old story? He said 'we have not the reverent feeling for the rainbow that a savage has, because we know how it's made. We have lost as much as we gained by prying into the matter.'

"We seem to have found the missing Library of Congress collection that Jefferson's friends claimed was destroyed when the Capitol was burned. Apparently they used its absence to justify transferring a hefty chunk of the taxpayer's money into the first presidential pension."

"Hmmm," Brooks said, "somehow that doesn't surprise me too much. It seems to me I've heard that hinted around before."

177

"Well done. Shows how old you are. You're right. Apparently back in 'olden days' it was pretty freely admitted, but then it became fashionable not even to hint at it. The latest reference to the fact I've been able to find in print was an oblique comment in the old black WPA Guide of 1937. Since then it seems to have been conveniently dropped from the literature. I suspect it was less that anybody was trying to hide it, than that various historians were accepting what their predecessors said without re-checking—and then spending their time adding on their own new stuff. The only hard suggestion was in a book by Johnston that was actually written around 1900. Mearns and Goodrum and Cole did new histories for each of their generations, but each of them was pushing some different point and didn't bother to replow their predecessors.

"The one thing I wished I had time for, was to find out what was said about it all at the time it happened. While we worship Jefferson now, in his day he was about as thoroughly hated by the New Englanders as Nixon was by Mary McGrory. The Federalists looked on the War of 1812 as Jefferson's war and cursed it like we did Vietnam. I wish I knew what they wrote home to their wives the day they had to vote all that free money for their worst enemy."

"Well, let's go down and look. Do you know the date of the vote?"

"Oh, sure. Who voted, how, and when, but I meant manuscripts—letters home, diaries, that sort of thing. You'd have to go all over the East Coast to get what I want."

"Ed, you insult the institution! All of that stuff has been microfilmed by whoever owns it and we all own what everybody else has. The sainted Massachusetts Historical Society has given us all pictures of everything the Founding Fathers gave them. Chapel Hill has shared miles of Southern papers. We have films of all the Calhoun and

Clay and Webster stuff—whoever the hell would have been there. You have a list of who voted?"

"Complete."

"Where is it?"

"Down in Crighton's office."

"Then we'll go by way of her shop when we've finished. Speaking of Crighton, we've got a real problem there. I don't know what we're going to do with her. When I first hired her now . . . what is it, three years ago? I intended to unload her as soon as I got the money she was supposed to generate from a new public image. Well, bless her heart, she got the image and we got the money, but by then she was so useful we just kept her on and on. From the library's point of view, we've been getting our money's worth, but I'm guilt-ridden that we're robbing her of her career youth. Pretty soon she'll be too old to move."

"She's conscious of it, too. What's the answer?"

"The textbooks say she's got to move on whether she wants to or not. We all did it, or we wouldn't be where we are now. The curse is, thirty years from now we all look back at a certain job we did wonderfully well and wonder why we left it. Peter was right. You go up till you get beyond your capacity, and then you're miserable the rest of your working life."

"Where would you have stopped?"

"A small college library. By now they'd have named the new building after me."

George laughed and said, "Let's go look into the letters."

"Here's the official vote," George said, pulling a sheet from Carson's pile. "In favor: seventy-seven Democrats and four Federalists. Against buying the Jefferson collection: fifty-three Federalists, fourteen Democrats, and one Republican. Jefferson offered his collection to the Congress on September 21. The Joint Committee on the Library brought the offer to the floor on October 7. The House voted in favor of it October 19, the Senate voted for it October 20. January 26 they authorized payment and the transfer of the funds. Presumably all we've got to do is look in the various diaries and letter files for the months of, say, September through February, and we've got it made. Right?"

"Sounds good to me. We'll simply compare the names of those who voted with our holding records—they're all alphabetical in a single printout—and we'll search whoever we find. Do you want the fors or the againsts?"

"You're the host. You get first choice."

"Then I'll take the folks who were against the idea. They ought to be more colorful," Brooks said as they started out the door.

They spent two hours side by side in front of a long wall lined with microfilm readers. The routine was load, fast forward; slow, frame-by-frame examination; rewind; and load the next reel. The evening passed as names were checked off: Calhoun, Lowndes, McLean, Desha. Some were enormous collections like the Breckinridge family with 849 reels and Daniel Webster with 41 reels of letters alone. Others were much smaller, but in every case they searched the fall and winter of 1814 and 1815. A strange pattern developed. The first sign of it appeared in the Webster papers.

"Brother! If we're going to find anything, it should be here," Brooks said. "Big Dan wrote his wife every even day and his son every odd day, and kept his foreman up to date on every political whisper. By the time you get through a week of these, you've heard every speech on the floor and know everything he ate, including snacks!"

Ten minutes later, he said, "Odd. Not a reference of any kind to the Library of Congress or to Jefferson's library. Jefferson catches hell every third paragraph, but not for his books. Strange."

"I've done five of the Virginians who voted for it, and there's not a mention of the vote—or even of the offer."

Another ten minutes and Brooks said, "I'm in the Brigham papers. Massachusetts. Those were the days. He's just told his wife to go ahead and hire a house girl. Going price: forty-five dollars a *year*."

An hour later, Brooks said, "This ought to be another gold mine. I've got Timothy Pickering writing home three and four letters a day. Here's one he's blaming Jefferson for the war, calls him 'cunning,' his foresight 'egregiously erroneous,' 'his views and designs have been incorrect and perverse.' Brother Pickering says Jefferson 'has read many books, and so far studied them as to be able to converse pleasantly on most every subject but without being profound in any.' Here's a letter of August 28 in which Pickering is delighted the Capitol was burned. He tells his wife, 'Should the enemy burn no more buildings, we shall be able to give Congress a very comfortable accommodation, and as republics have no business with palaces the accommodation will perhaps be more in character.' He's going to blow a gasket when he's asked to give twenty-five thousand dollars to his favorite enemy."

Twenty minutes later Brooks said, "Odd. I'm into February and no mention of the collection good, bad, or sideways. Yet Pickering seems to have commented on every last subject they discussed in the chambers. What are we seeing here?"

"Beats me. I've done all the yes people we had and there was no mention of the offer or the purchase of the Jefferson books. I kept expecting someone to preen themselves on how well they had done for good old Tom. But even more, your enemies should have been outraged. No reference at all?"

"Nothing. Do you suppose there really was a vote?

181

Could this have been like those phantom speeches that fill the *Record* now? Or maybe even more like the pairing votes, where neither of the members are in the city, but both get their names on record by leaving a yes-no vote with the clerk to be entered at appropriate times."

"Presumably that would mean the majority party Democrats took a poll in the hall or in some party caucus, got agreement, and just arbitrarily said 'even if we put down a no for every Federalist, we've still got enough if we all vote yes. Let's not get everybody stirred up with a public vote.' And they did it all on paper in the clerk's office."

"There were a few maverick votes in the noes, but only four in the yeses. Damn strange. Very odd."

"Why wouldn't there have been more questions about what happened to the original three thousand books?" Brooks asked.

"God knows. I suppose you can write a scenario that runs something like: the British are coming to take the city. Everybody runs around trying to save the official papers of the departments—State, Treasury, War—and the stuff is put in houses and barns and village churches all over the neighboring countryside. There it stays until the British go away, but since they'd burned all of the public buildings, there was no place to bring it all back to in Washington. So it would have been months before a lot of it reappeared—there sure wouldn't have been a place to hold three thousand books. Incidentally, when I was running the history of the period, I was amused to discover that there was serious consideration given to abandoning the city and rebuilding the Capitol and the White House someplace else—probably Philadelphia. The hot summers and the miasmic damp had turned everybody off with 'Foggy Bottom.' A bunch of local businessmen hurriedly put up a temporary brick Capitol to forestall everybody moving out for good. Anyhow, once Jefferson's friends filed that report saying 'the library was destroyed' it could be that nobody wasted any time looking around for where the books *might* have been lying for the past months. But who knows? Very strange."

The two men struggled to their feet, both stiff from fixed focus on the screens. They carried the trays of boxes back to the return desk and left the room, still bemused, trying to account for the singular lack of productive results from their labors.

"I apologize for having led you down such a fruitless path," George said.

"Nonsense. It was fascinating. It's always refreshing to be reminded of how important all the things those folks were writing about with such concern were to them—and how little they mattered in the overall scheme of things. If I didn't so enjoy my own despair, I couldn't help but notice the parallel between their problems and my own. They were all bedeviled by public concerns *and* family matters. I presume your letters were as full of panic as mine were over the coming loss of New Orleans and with it the Mississippi and all the West. Not a single one that I read even considered the possibility that Jackson might beat the British and drive the enemy away. And how did it come out? Jackson lost some eighty men and the British suffered two thousand casualties and left the continent for good."

George laughed, "Something like that. Yes, it does sort of put our difficulties into perspective."

"And speaking of the way things come out," Brooks said as they started around the marble banisters of the Great Hall, "what ever happened to that splendid woman you brought with you to the concert here last year? An extraordinarily regal lady with a charming look of wit and intelligence. I always wondered how you got her to come out in public with you."

"You mean Alexa Lehman. Yes, we correspond and I

phone her once a month or so. Right now she's in Vienna tying up some family estate business."

"The rumor mill said she's as rich as sin. Is that true?"

"I have a suspicion she is. She lives very well. Beautiful apartment out on Massachusetts by the park. She travels a great deal."

"Crighton says she's marvelously self-sufficient."

"Yes, she lives every minute of every day."

"And your age?"

"Yes."

"She was stunning. What are you waiting for? Crighton said you and she had a warm rapport."

"How does that Wilde quote go? 'Men marry because they are tired; women because they are curious. Both are disappointed.'"

"Too true to be funny."

"So what are you going to do about Crighton?"

They were back in the director's office, and Brooks answered, "Well, as I see it, I've got three choices. One, just let it roll on like it is and leave all movement up to her. Two, arbitrarily move her to another job in the library—maybe as my own executive assistant. And three, terminate her job and force her out on the street to create two points on a career ladder."

"Makes sense. Which way are you going to go?"

"I'll have to think a bit more about it."

"Marvelous. Have you ever thought of going into politics? You could create a commission to study it, and demand a full report and conclusion in three years—whether they were ready or not."

"I like it. Let me get a pencil and you say that again very slowly."

They both shook their heads in wry despair.

Chapter 25

"THERE, that's better," Crighton said, having removed her shoes and hose in the bedroom and reappearing barefooted in the living room. Carson was sitting on the floor, leaning against the couch, and Crighton flounced down on the cushions above him. She spun around to lean against one arm with her legs stretched out in bliss. "God, that is an improvement. How can two shoe straps constrain the entire body?"

"The same way a necktie changes a man's personality. It must go back to the cave. The strap around the neck showed who was the slave. The shoes showed who was in charge, but with it went the responsibilities of authority." He reflected on this thought for a moment and said, "Forget it. I don't think there's a paper there."

He looked up at her. "Woman, you are outrageously sexy when you're barefooted. When you patter around, you look like a smooth little six-year-old completely at peace with the world. How beautifully you are designed."

"Has it ever occurred to you that everyone looks sexy to you, and that any female is properly designed?"

"That is not true. You are the only woman I ever met who so completely satisfies all my requirements. You come together so gracefully and all your planes match just right. Your colors are great and your textures are sublime. Have I ever—"

"Did you ever think how little use you'd have for me if I was ugly? Even very ordinary, according to your standards?"

"'Iffy questions.' The females' most dangerous—and indefensible—weapon. But yes. I'd love to be with you no matter how you looked. You're interesting, intelligent, have a great sense of humor. It just happens that having all that, packaged as you are, is absolutely mind-shattering. Crighton Jones, I am very fond of you. When are you going to marry me?"

"Ah, Steve," she said, more seriously than usual. "If I could only get myself organized and get set in some firm direction, I could deal with that, but—"

"Never mind the 'deal' with it. It's very simple: does it sound like fun? Would life be better with me or without me? All this organization and dealing . . . we could do it together! Come on! We could bounce all your indecisions back and forth and have twice the fun."

"But until I'm sure what I want for *myself*, I can't *share* anything. I'd always feel like you'd cheated me out of something and made me split everything by halves. I've got to get my all and *then* I can give you parts with an open hand. Don't you understand?"

"In a word: no. But looking at the bright side, as is my longtime wont, I note we got through all those words without a single 'I'd rather be dead than. . . .' You see, we progress! All I've got to do is convince you that life would be ten times more pleasurable, with brighter colors and richer strings and gayer laughter, with me than all by yourself. You do understand, don't you? Your choice is between me and no one else, ever? That is an accepted given, is it not?"

Crighton laughed. "Yes, Steve. I promise it's you or nobody. Ever."

He turned toward her and ran his fingertips along her temples and into her hair. "Thank you, princess. The glass mountain is high and steep, but bless your heart, you're worth it."

He proceeded to demonstrate the depth of his conviction in gentle, unhurried detail.

Considerably later in the evening, Crighton was scrambling eggs on the stove while Carson built up a plateful of buttered toast. He turned away from this task to contemplate a shelf of coffee cups, trying to decide between utilitarian mugs versus some graceful, handled affairs that clearly required saucers to maintain their dignity. He opted to the saucered design. This was an occasion, he decided, that demanded class throughout.

"Woman," he said, "was Park really serious about charging Brent?"

"Oh, he acts like it, but fortunately he can't find him so he can't make a fool of himself for the moment."

"Where do you think he's gone?"

"Nowhere. He's probably either upstairs in the attic or down with the books. He'll turn up when he wants to— though they'd better keep a sharp eye after dark. It doesn't make any difference. Brent didn't do it."

"You're really set on that, aren't you?"

"Of course. I don't know why you're all so eager to hang it on that turkey. The only way he'd have had the nerve to hit her was out of hysteria, and then he'd have had to deal with the body. By that time he'd have come completely apart and be lying around in little pieces. No, I'm increasingly convinced it's Grace Fairchild, but for all the right reasons. I suspect Steele *should* have been taken out, and if you think about it, there really was no way it could be done other than this."

"You don't believe in the sure hand of the law?"

"What she was fighting was exposure, not theft. She'd found something that would tarnish the reputations of a Founding Father, a dignified institution, and a long-respected Virginia family. Any legal assault on Steele would have laid the whole schmeir out in public, and she'd have done the precise thing she was trying to avoid. No, somebody had to silence Steele before she said another word."

"The *bookkeeper* meets all the formal requirements, you know," Carson said. "I suspect he'd love to get even with his employers, he's got roughly the same access as Fairchild has, and no doubt his messing around with the assets could have turned up a record of the books in the cellar. Hmmm . . . if he was going after the books himself and found Steele butting in, he could have knocked her off to prevent her ruining the deal—but how would he have known what she was up to? Eavesdropping on something? Does the phone to the house go through that office? No. No, I don't think he's involved. He doesn't seem to have any links with anything or anybody—he's like a free-floating cork. Anyway, he came from hell-and-gone in California, not Virginia."

"California? Wait a minute. That came up in my conversation with Fairchild. Uh . . . got it. She told me that one of the Fairfax family went west during the Gold Rush and settled in Marin County. Second or third generation of Lord Fairfax kin."

"That's too late to be mixed up in this mess. The Fairfaxes had been gone forty years before the books got in the basement."

"But the descendants might have had some links to Belvoir—old family home, or something?"

"More to the point, I suppose," Carson said, "is that

Phelps actually does come from Marin County where he worked at the Herrington Library and Art Gallery. But that's awfully thin. It was Steele who was murdered—a complete outsider. How would Phelps have known what she was up to?"

"He certainly would have access to the office files. Park is convinced that Brent put the Porsche keys and stuff in Grace's file drawer. If the bookkeeper were involved, it would have been even easier for him to do it than Elliott—but the keys are the easiest to explain simply by Grace shoving them there herself. They're her files."

"You don't think there's a chance Fairchild was working with Elliott, do you?" Carson asked. "Fairchild wanted silence, Brent wanted quiet water for selling those books before the house was handed over. Could Fairchild have thought it up and Brent carried it out?"

"That is just barely possible. One of the weakest parts of Fairchild's story is her claim that she still hasn't seen the books and that she never mentioned any of this to the ladies. It's hard to believe she's been on the grounds for a year and hasn't accomplished either one. She might have talked to the family and she and Brent got the assassination all set up awaiting the arrival of Madame Steele. Then again, she might have talked just to Brent and the two of them cooked it all up for opposite reasons. They both had plenty of opportunity to do the deed, and neither is completely covered by an alibi. Fairchild could have killed the woman while Brent was in New York. Brent could have moved the car while Fairchild was giving a tour. And they both could have carried the body around in the night—together. Hmmm. If this were so, where would it lead us?"

At which point the phone rang in the living room, and Crighton turned off the fire. "Why don't you serve this stuff, while I see who that is."

By the time she returned, Steve had the kitchen table

covered with food and was looking at his handiwork with satisfaction. Magnificent, he thought, could be the cover of *Fine Food and Expensive Wine.*

"Can you believe who that was!" Crighton shouted. "Alexa Lehman! She's back from Austria and was simply checking in—she had no idea Dr. George was here. She was overjoyed and is insisting we all come out for brunch tomorrow. It's absolutely great. I love it!"

"That is a good thing," Carson said. "That is a splendid woman. It'll do George good."

"What would it take to get him to ask her to marry him?"

"Oh? What's with the 'let's get everybody married' bit? Great for everyone else but not for you? You ought to be shaken. But you're right. They'd both be happier together, and that is a condition that can be spread all over the place, beginning here. Brunch at Madame Lehman's—I can taste those croissants from here. Not to mention the silent maid and the baroque silver trays. That is the way the Lord intended me to live. Have you called George?"

"No. I told her where she could find him. It'll do 'em both good."

"At least you have the capacity to see how the whole can be greater than the parts. Now if we can bring this truth a little closer to home, there may be hope yet."

He kissed her gently, and she said, "Shut up and eat."

Chapter 26

SATURDAY morning. Everyone was spread around Alexa Lehman's living room. The difference between this apartment and most apartments, Carson thought, was the way you could see so far before you ran into a wall. You could look across wide, low rooms into more wide, low rooms surrounded by wide, low windows. And the carpeting flowed serenely as far as the eye could see. He let his fingers trace the smooth parts of the brocade on the chair arm and he inhaled deeply. Lovely. The place even smelled elegant, he thought. Just the kind of ambience I was intended for.

Lehman was wearing chic, belted street clothes. Stylishly coifed, she looked like she was on her way to a morning of Fifth Avenue shopping. The silent maid, even as Carson had remembered her, had passed around silver trays of delicate, enormously caloric pastries and was now replenishing coffee cups from a Queen Anne pot.

"All right, Edward," Alexa Lehman was saying, "that Scheherazade performance you were staging last night was just barely tolerable." She turned toward the other two.

"Do I understand that you all have gotten yourselves involved in another murder? Edward stubbornly refused to give me any details until we were all together. I recall Lieutenant Conrad telling us that all crimes can be explained by 'money, booze, or sex.' Does that maxim apply here?"

"Not sex, not booze, and money only maybe," George replied. "Now that we have a quorum, let me bring you up to date. This puzzle is hung on an intriguing historical incident." He proceeded through an extensive and detailed review of the steps that had led them to that moment, and concluded by saying, "and we now find ourselves with equally good cases against the roommate, Grace Fairchild, and the nephew, Elliott Brent. Equally good but involving totally different motives."

Lehman smiled and said, "Do you remember that experiment Josephine Tey describes in *The Daughter of Time*? She tells how someone took a broad sample of famous English crimes and got the photograph of the presiding judge and the guilty accused. Then they asked a hundred people which was which. According to Tey, not a single person failed to select the guilty man. Does one of your suspects look guiltier than the other?"

"Oh, my yes," Carson jumped in. "The man is a sleazy pip-squeak who could be fencing Xeroxed twenties in dark alleys. The woman is an aristocratic, intelligent, principled citizen—"

"With a very good figure," Crighton broke in.

"That too," Carson conceded. "Manifestly innocent as the driven snow.

"No. Seriously," Carson said, "I think your 'money' is the answer here. Given: the Brents—the women, not the nephew—decide to give the plantation to the state to protect themselves from ruinous estate taxes. This gets the women out of some onerous obligations, but leaves Elliott neutered. In the house he is something . . . somebody.

The house gives him standing. With house gone and him in a condo, he's just like anybody else in the elevator. He's desperate. He's got to have money and importance and an independent income—not crumbs from his aunts. And the answer is in the basement. The family secret just a floor away. To the Brents, it is something to be hidden to cover a questionable raid on the Treasury a hundred and fifty years ago. To him, it's a half-million dollars that will compensate him for the loss of standing. He goes to New York, starts the rounds of the booksellers, and is cheered to find both interest and potential commitment.

"He comes home to find the savage Steele threatening to tell the world of the Brent family's duplicity unless she gets some real money to keep her silent. Junior doesn't give a damn about the money—which'll come out of his aunts anyway—but he doesn't want anything that might queer the sale of those books. He gets Steele somewhere alone—in the book cellar? in one of the outbuildings?—and knocks her off. After Fairchild leaves, he takes everything out of her purse that could identify her, puts her under the floorboards, and starts on the permanent grave in anticipation of resolving it all the following night.

"But he gets to thinking. What if Steele told somebody where she was going and what she was going to do? He decides to set up a scene in which it would look like Steele had gotten the money she was after, drove to the airport, and took off for parts unknown. He moves the car, hides the keys and driver's license in the back of Fairchild's files for insurance, and he's reestablished a clear path. Now all he has to do is bring off the sale before everybody moves out and the mansion goes to the state. Motivation? Eliminate a threat to his retirement plan. Opportunity? All over the place. Means? A hammer or a brick, and grounds full of holes and floorboards and sites he'd grown up with all his life."

Crighton responded sweetly, "Other than that it's all

one hundred percent wrong, it's a beautiful theory that takes care of everything he can think of. Madame Lehman, the guy he's talking about is a shallow, effete lightweight that not only couldn't manage anything as complex as Steve is trying to sell, he simply doesn't care that much about anything—not even money. No, I'm sorry to say, the person who did it and is going to have to pay for it is a really admirable woman of style and intelligence—and unfortunately, a set of ethics.

"Grace Fairchild is acutely aware that she started all this mess. She rolled the rock off the initial indiscretion—hiding the missing books that weren't really missing at all . . . spending public money under false pretenses—and with it she opened everything up. She knew she was going to leave a film over all sorts of good things—a respected patriot, a great institution, and a revered family. So far as she could see, the only way she could put the scum back in the bottle was to kill the person who knew about it all and was going to tell. Although she says she never saw Steele, I think she did. She surprised her from behind, and hit her with something hard. She waited till dark, carried the body to her office, put it under the floor, and went out to the garden and dug that grave. All that talk about looking all over the grounds and down by the river was to cover herself in case someone saw her going out to do the digging. Dawn came too early to run the risk of moving the body that day, so she let everything stand until the following, and we all barged in and screwed things up.

"What worries me is that if we don't do something, she'll kill herself as the only way out. But if we do do something, we end up getting her hung and she probably doesn't deserve it! Yet even worse, if we do nothing, that policeman is liable to think like Steve does, and we'll end up with yet another miscarriage of justice with that miserable nephew in jeopardy for all the wrong reasons. What a mess!"

Madame Lehman was frowning with concern. "My goodness, Edward. This is serious. How did you let things go this far? Not only have you got to find justice, you've got to prevent injustice. It sounds like you're going to do real damage either going forward or doing nothing. How did you get into this fix?"

"I protest! Respected lady, don't blame us! We didn't start this. We're trying to sort it out!"

She looked at George and waved a hand toward Steve and Crighton. "So which way do you lean? Which explanation do you support?"

George replied, "I'm terrified to say it, but I'm leaning toward the thought that they both did it together, for opposite reasons, but ended up sharing the task. I suspect Fairchild did indeed go there to forestall Steele. I suspect she told Elliott, recognizing an unprincipled ally, and the two were waiting for Steele's arrival. They just passed the steps back and forth between them."

Carson joined the conversation. "We were at exactly that point when Alexa called last night, but it wasn't clear how you'd prove it, and whose idea it was."

He stopped suddenly and interrupted himself. "Wait a minute. Is it possible we've got the leverage on this all wrong? We're assuming that anybody'd care enough about this book business to knock somebody off. Hell, would anyone really have been willing to pay money to keep somebody quiet in this day and age? I assured the Jones here that they would, but I'm beginning to wonder. Would the Brents really have forked over to keep the Steele shut up? Would the F.F.V. really care enough to drive Grace Fairchild off the deep end?"

"Oh, yes. Yes, indeed," Alexa said with conviction. "And I think you're right to look for what matters most to whom here. As you've painted it, you can make a remarkably equal case between the two individuals—but they are two very different cases. Do you all realize what a different set of values you're working with? You could almost say your choice of the murderer mirrors the American and the European psyches. The Brent man comes across as the personification of the American way gone awry. He seems to have great entrepreneurial spirit, total independence from tradition, and the ability to deal with the events of the moment with alacrity. I think you call it being fast on his feet.

"The lady sounds much more European. She seems terribly concerned about what those books 'mean,' what they stand for in some mystical sense, and she seems driven to return everything to the status quo."

Carson said, "So you're saying that Brent is reality. He wants those bucks so bad he'd really do something about it. Fairchild is just worried about cloudland in theory."

"No, no. Not at all. The grip of tradition could be just as firm on the daughter of a modern Virginian—"

"She's what they call an F.F.V. here," Crighton said. "They're—"

"Oh, yes," Alexa nodded. "I've worked with many of them on my volunteer things, and they're much more like my European friends than many of my American. Let me explain. What seems to make the difference is the American conviction that each one of you, individually, is all that matters. Life begins with you personally. Your own parents teach you this. You can do anything you yourselves want. It is up to you to make your own life. Nothing that went before need be considered, you are not to blame for your ancestors' mistakes—no one will hold your father's sins against you. Your father's riches will probably not be available to you either! Your family must not help you too much or they will rob you of the triumph of your own making. You are all indeed islands to be populated

196

and governed as you alone decide. It sounds to me like your Elliott Brent plays by these rules with no thought of anyone but himself.

"Now your Miss Fairchild seems quite typical of the patrician Virginians I know. They don't think of themselves as individual islands, they see themselves more as part of the stream—endless, slowly moving, going where the river has always gone. They know the sins of their fathers are indeed clouding their lives, and they know any sins they commit will cloud their successors'. That poor Fairchild girl can't just 'go home and forget' about all this. Home is where it will matter the most."

"Are you sure that's true of our century?" Carson asked. "Maybe Victorian times, but—"

"No. Right now. Let me tell you something about my own family," Alexa continued. "My family was very minor nobility. They received the title in the early 1700s and were a part of the court until its dissolution in World War I." She smiled wryly, "A rather distant part of the court, way back against the far wall, but a titled family nevertheless, and—" she suddenly leaned forward and tapped the palm of her hand, "I know every mistake my ancestors made for two hundred years. Every indiscretion, every bad choice, every embarrassment has been carefully passed from generation to generation. I know only a few of the triumphs and the positive things my kin ever did, but I know every error they ever committed right back to the von. No, I suspect Miss Fairchild knows she has committed an unforgivable sin against the rules by which her family plays. It will magnify her decisions and exaggerate her actions quite out of proportion to the daily choices most people make."

The room went silent as everyone applied these values to the facts they held. Crighton was nodding in agreement, Carson was skeptical, and George was staring into space, running a finger tip back and forth across his lips.

"If what you say is true—and you do make a convincing case," he said, seemingly reflecting as he talked, "our problem becomes an exercise in assessing who believed what about this affair and how strongly they felt. I wish we could get Grace Fairchild and Elliott Brent face to face—eyeball to eyeball. Maybe we could play one against the other and see if we could frighten them into revealing what really matters to them and how much." He pulled at his throat for a moment, and then said, "Where do you suppose Brent is right now?"

"Right there in the house," Crighton answered. "I don't think he's ever left it. I suspect every time the cops come around he slides into that doorless room in the cellar. Back with the sailcloth and down the hole! If you really want to flush him out, go talk to the sisters Brent. Imply something new has happened or we've learned something. He'll appear like magic."

Carson grinned. "She's probably right, and you could pick up Fairchild on the way in."

"The sisters Brent . . . I'm afraid I can think of no way of getting onto that second floor," George said ruefully. "Anyone got any ideas?"

"Do you mean how can you get into the house?" Lehman asked. "When did you last see the sisters?"

"Not since my walk with them by the river."

Lehman laughed. "My, the chatelaines certainly have you intimidated, Edward. I can't believe you can't even think of how to meet them. What magic do these ladies have over you? I must see if I can borrow their wand." She looked toward the dining room and said, "Phyllis. Would you please call Information and get the number for the Belvoir Mansion in . . . what is the nearest town?"

Crighton said, "Fairfax County should do it."

A few moments later, Madame Lehman was speaking into the phone at a writing desk by the side of the room. "Miss Brent? I apologize for calling you without an intro-

198

duction, but something quite urgent has come up about that unfortunate matter that occurred at Belvoir the other day, and I think I'm obligated to bring it to your attention. My name is Alexa Lehman. I serve on the Fine Arts Commission and the National Board for the Preservation of Antiquities, and I think we may have mutual friends who can vouch for me." There was a pause and she said, "How very gracious of you. Actually the sooner the better, I'm afraid . . . that is wonderful. Four of us will be there very shortly, if that would be possible. Thank you so much, we'll come as quickly as we can."

She replaced the phone and turned toward George with her eyes twinkling. "Now that wasn't so hard was it? Whose car do you want to use? Mine's in the garage downstairs, if you want to take it."

Crighton said, "Carson's driven there enough, he's finally figured out where it is. Let's take his. It'll make him feel useful. Come on, Schliemann. On your feet."

While Carson had a sense of things moving past him a bit faster than he was moving himself, Crighton was smiling with an odd air of satisfaction, and George seemed to be far away, preoccupied, deeply lost in thought.

Chapter 27

THE trip from Washington to Belvoir was unusually quiet for four such voluble figures. They seemed to be preoccupied with the puzzle, while George appeared increasingly irritated as he brooded on the situation. His expression changed from frowns to grim determination as he stared out the window, apparently fixing on nothing that passed.

They arrived at the plantation shortly after noon, and Crighton went directly to the guide's room, assuming that Fairchild would have finished her second morning tour. Although the building was open, there was no one there. She rejoined the rest of the group and they walked toward the house, three of them waiting for instructions from George on how to proceed.

"Any particular role you wish me to play, Edward?" Lehman asked.

George seemed to pull his attention back from whatever he had been thinking about and said, "Uh, yes. I think I'd be grateful if you just introduced us and got things settled down, and then let me take over. I have an idea. It may not work, but I don't see how it can do any more damage than what we've done already."

"The woman said to come to a little door on the ground floor over at the side," Lehman said. "It must be over there."

As they moved around the house to the left they discovered an unobtrusive entrance they had not noticed before, upstaged as it was by the two splendid, fan-vaulted porches on the front and back. They also found Fairchild talking to two visitors in the front garden, and Crighton hurried ahead to catch her. She excused herself from her audience and followed Crighton back, clearly surprised and somewhat apprehensive. Crighton could not tell whether she was seeing distress over their invading the private space of the second floor, or concern over the reason for the meeting.

The group, now five strong, followed Alexa Lehman to the little door, and she tapped quietly as she had been instructed. Sarah Brent appeared almost at once and invited them in as graciously as if they had been summoned by engraved invitation. Lehman conducted the introductions on the threshold, and the group followed the woman through the door and up two floors of exceedingly narrow back stairs. The passage was dimly lit by a pair of medallion windows set high in the walls.

Sarah Brent conversed cordially as she led the ascent. "As you can imagine," she said, "these were the servants' stairs. They link all the floors so the servants could come and go from their own quarters without being seen—and they could carry linen and water up and down without going through the formal rooms. I am always amused at the inadvertent class separation they provided. In almost every age, the gentlewomen of the house wore farthingales or hoops or bustles. These stairs are so narrow and the turnings so abrupt that the owners couldn't possibly have navigated them. Watch your step. They are still more utilitarian than graceful."

They came out on the second floor and walked down a hall to a large sitting room that sat atop the center hall below. A high ceiling cut by several dormers made the room light, airy, and comfortable. Chintz-covered furniture gave it the feel of a 1920s country estate.

"How attractive this room is," Lehman said. "I expected formal antiques; this is comfortably lovely."

"Yes, the public floor is completely accurate to the time period of the house, but we all live up here—everyone has a bedroom and a sitting room, and it works very well."

At this point Martha Brent joined them and was introduced, and in the midst of this, Elliott Brent appeared from the opposite hall and slouched against the door frame, acknowledging his introductions with a casual nod. Crighton exchanged an I-told-you-so look with Carson.

"Do sit down, everyone."

Sarah Brent was playing the gracious Virginia hostess, deliberately avoiding any reference to the purpose of the meeting until the guests would bring it up. Sarah tended to be somewhat muscular and moved with the vigor of a hiker or a horsewoman. Martha was thinner, taller, and more aristocratic.

Alexa Lehman glanced at George to see if he had any new signal to express, and finding none, took over the "settling down" duties she had been assigned.

"That image of all those women and those stairs was marvelous," she said. "I was particularly taken by it because of something that happened to me only last week in Vienna.

"My family has had a modest town house just off the Herrengasse near the Hofburg for many years, and I was over clearing out some furniture and things. There is a porch arrangement at the front that sits a few steps above the sidewalk, and it has an iron railing across the front that goes down on either side to the street. I was leaning across the railing in blue jeans and a sweater, trying to see if something had been put in the lorry, and I got to thinking how I must look hanging out across the sidewalk."

She laughed quietly. "And then I suddenly got this picture of a woman leaning over that same railing looking into a hansom cab to see if the doctor had come. Of a woman in Empire clothing handing a letter to an officer going out to meet Napoleon. Of a woman in a powdered wig giving instructions to the coachman. Always leaning across that same iron railing. It was quite unnerving, and the images kept recurring all day long—as I was unscrewing electric light fixtures, would you believe?" She laughed again and then asked, "Do you have a picture of an endless stream of people living in this house?"

Martha stepped into the conversation. "Oh, yes, not just 'people,' but specific women. Women who did specific things after the Revolution and after the War between the States, and so on."

"Are these women tied to the house? Like Scarlett's love for Tara in your marvelous *Gone with the Wind* story?"

Sarah Brent responded, "Not the house. I don't think any of us has any particular feeling for the house. It's simply the place where these people lived. It could be any house. The people are much more real."

Lehman said, "I agree. The Herrengasse place is simply the place where things occurred. The house did not 'see' them. It has no personality of its own."

She paused, and Crighton sensed that she was about to turn to George to see if that was enough, when George cleared his throat to signal he was ready to take over. Crighton wondered which of the two suspects he would try to break down first—and was therefore surprised when he turned directly toward the hostess and spoke in an unusually cold and impersonal voice.

"Miss Brent," he said, looking magisterially at Sarah, "we appreciate your letting us visit you. The reason we are here concerns the murder of that woman earlier in the week. I presume your nephew has kept you abreast of our involvement in the matter, so we need not go into that. There are, however, some aspects of the situation about which, I suspect, you are not aware. We have had the advantage of speaking to the police and to some of the people concerned about factors that you would not have had the opportunity to hear. The fact is that the situation has gone much further than you may have realized, and it seemed appropriate to make you aware of it."

He turned toward Martha. "I believe you may wish to change your mode of action. The way you chose to deal with the situation as it developed might have been—from your point of view, at least—appropriate at the time. It is no longer. Matters are rapidly building toward an explosion that will cause much greater damage than what has already occurred, and I believe you will wish to forestall it. To be harsh, I think 'cutting your losses' may be the appropriate phrase."

He turned back to Sarah. "As we were coming down from Washington, I was wondering how to express the situation to you, and then as we came out of that long corridor of trees and burst on to the tableau of the mansion, the whole point of the matter struck me. There is a sense of continuity here that goes from history to history, generation to generation, people to people. Inexorably. Unstoppably. You had hinted at it when we spoke down by the river.

"I was struck by how the events of this week must have confronted you, and I sensed the successive dilemmas they must have posed. You were not asking what was the right thing to do when that woman called you about the Jefferson books—yes, we know about them, and we think we have some sense of what they mean to you and your family. And that is the real point here. What you have been asking yourselves over and over in the past days is, What will what we do look like to the rest of the family, to the family of the next generation, and the next? And you decided it was all simply too much to be borne. You tried to bury what had occurred. Bury, as it happens, in every sense. And, from your point of view, it might have been worth the try, but I tell you both: it has fallen out that what your successors will hear is far worse than what you were trying to prevent.

"This girl—Miss Fairchild—is much too close to suicide. Strangely enough, given what she has to deal with, that is a very sane and rational solution for her troubles. If she doesn't kill herself, she may well be seized for the murder of that extortionist. Your nephew there is equally threatened with a murder charge that will not only ruin him, but leave an unnecessary and an unjust shadow on the name of Brent. Your family seems to have gotten away with history's failing memory on the books, but it will not on a murder. This violent incident will not evaporate into the mists of time. Your initial decision is sweeping in larger and larger circles to damage more people more savagely than you could have imagined. If I have read this story right, there are indeed difficulties ahead for you, but none so bad as they will be if you do nothing and let others now make your choices for you. Hear me: your gamble did not pay off. You are on the threshold of unprincipled, dishonorable destruction. You must put a limit to the damage you have done."

He leaned back, leaving the room in dead silence, broken by a throaty gasp from Elliott Brent. "Hey! Watch it. What the fuck is he trying to pull?" Looking directly at the two sisters, he said, "Don't say anything. They don't know anything. Don't give everything away on absolutely nothing. Shut up. Shut up, do you hear me?"

Sarah Brent shot him a withering glance, and said, "Don't ever tell me to shut up. Don't you ever tell me to do anything, you fool. You shut up. Not another word." She turned toward Martha, and said in a firm voice, "Well, we were prepared for this. I think the man is right. What do you think?"

The two women looked at each other in the silent room. Crighton was sensitive to the sun streaming in on the bright chintz slip covers, the white muslin curtains brilliant with light, the air of pleasant ease marred by the harsh tension of a decision that would have to be lived with for years to come.

Martha nodded slowly and the nephew shouted, "No, no! They're tricking you. They don't know anything!"

Sarah spoke. "That despicable woman called us and then came to visit us and we, of course, threw her out without a moment's hesitation. That night we heard someone trying to break into the cellar through a window. In the dark, we saw someone prying the grill off and we hit whoever it was. It proved to be that woman, and rather than starting a degrading fuss over a trivial matter, we thought it best simply to bury her and be done with it. As you suggest, it may have been a mistake, but it was worth a try. We will now call in my brother, who is one of an army of Brent lawyers, and he will take the matter to a courtroom of some judge with standards and traditions and a knowledge of our family. Since it was all so accidental and unpremeditated, it should be resolved without further difficulty."

"You use the word 'we,'" George said. "Who will take responsibility for the death?"

"We all will. Equally."

"What are you saying?" Elliott Brent shouted. "I wasn't even here. I came home to find you two had knocked her off and you got me to help cover it up. I'm not going to take the rap for—"

"Shut up, I tell you," Sarah said harshly. "If you want any help from the family to keep you out of jail, you will not say another word. Not a word. You have been told for the last time." She turned back to George. "We will all accept a share of responsibility for an unfortunate, un-premeditated result of trying to defend the mansion against a break-in by an unprincipled interloper."

"Very well," George replied. "Needless to say, we will

be obligated to report this discussion to the policeman in charge of the case, so no one must leave the area. I would urge you to use the next half an hour to contact your attorneys—at once. Note: no one here has mentioned the antecedents of the books, specifically, to the authorities. They were told that there were rare books involved, but the Jefferson connection has not been spelled out." He looked directly at the Brents. "I believe that condition can be preserved, if you so wish."

"Thank you. And I recognize that what you are saying is that if we digress from the present understanding, you will not hesitate to spell it out publicly."

George nodded. "You understand our thoughts. And no one is implicated other than you three?"

"That is correct."

George looked at his friends. "Is there anything anyone wishes to add?"

Steve and Crighton gave a look that seemed to suggest they wouldn't touch this one with a ten-foot pole, and Alexa Lehman appeared to be having trouble repressing a smile. "No," she said, "I think you have expressed what was required."

Edward George turned back toward the Brents and stood up. "Then I think we should leave you. I am distressed to think of the difficulties that lie ahead for you, but I am certain you are up to them—most of them, you recognize, were brought on by yourselves and your family. Would you like us to go out the way we came?"

The Brents rose with the rest and Sarah said, "No, no. You must go out through the Great Hall. As you yourself said, there have been many others of my family who went down these steps carrying concerns equally as difficult. We will survive. Please follow me."

They descended the great staircase with Crighton frantically searching the sailcloth floor covering, looking for the telltale outline of a door to the cellar. There was none apparent through the complicated, painted design.

They reached the huge doors and as Sarah unlocked them and pushed them open she said, "Thank you all for your consideration." Thank God, Carson thought, she is not shaking our hands. The four walked out, and the door was locked noisily behind them.

Shortly thereafter they were all packed into the guide's office, where they had found Park suitably astonished at their presence. It being Saturday, there was no sign of Phelps, and Crighton concluded he must work a five-day week. George introduced Madame Lehman and brought the officer up to date on the situation.

"That's it in a nutshell, lieutenant," he concluded. "You now know about as much about it as we do. The idea that it was all an unpremeditated, spur-of-the-moment act is almost certain nonsense. Every step they took was either carefully thought out, or was set into a premeditated matrix designed to achieve a deliberate end, but that will be up to the legal system to deal with—unsuccessfully, I suspect, but we do what we can. I presume you'll want to get up there and make things official before they change their minds. Why don't we get out of your way, in case you want to call headquarters or whatever."

He meant "for instructions and reinforcements," but felt it tactless to say so. Park expressed his thanks in a slightly stunned manner, and the rest walked out onto the lawn, brilliant in the midday sun.

Grace Fairchild's eyes were flooded with tears. "I don't know how to—"

"Then don't," Crighton cut in firmly. "It gives us almost as much pleasure to see it resolved as it does you. All we ask is, will you please look us right in the eye and tell us honestly that you had nothing to do with the killing."

"As God is my witness," she replied intensely, "I knew

208

no more about it than you did. I kept coming on things after they happened. I did nothing other than open up the whole mess with that research about the Jefferson pay-off. It's all been absolutely horrible."

"And now, Dr. George," said Crighton, "you owe us one massive explanation. That was tremendous in there. But how—or when—or why or something! What made you decide that it was they that'd done it?"

"Hah!" George said somewhat grimly, "Elliott Brent was right, of course. It was all a massive bluff, but I thought I might either get a rational resolution or someone would panic. Hunh. I lucked out. Miss Fairchild, can we go somewhere to talk?"

"How about the old kitchen over there?" Fairchild replied.

They hurried to it, and the guide unhooked ropes and shoved stands aside, so everyone could drop onto benches and stools.

"Well!" George said with a sigh. "We all nearly had the answer, but everything was so even—nothing or nobody stood above the flat surface. Who was the *most* likely? What motivation *really* was enough? Everything was as possible as everything else.

"What kept troubling me was that someone had had to kill that very vital woman who had made such an impression on Crighton. Someone had had to reach out at arm's length and strike her down. Killing is not casual, even if we talk coolly about it in the living room, yet none of the folks involved seemed to care that much. Crighton kept telling us that nephew Elliott didn't have the guts to do away with someone with his own hands. And forgive us, Grace Fairchild, you had all the rational reasons for having killed the woman—motive and opportunity and all those sorts of things—but, my dear, there was too much Hamlet about you. If you were going to kill the woman to shut her up, you should have done it as quickly as you learned of her stealing your secret. Or of learning of her intent to make it public. Or on learning that she was coming to the mansion. Or . . . there were too many 'well not now, I'd better wait to be sures.' No, there simply wasn't enough malicious fibre in either you or Elliott Brent.

"And then, Alexa, you gave us that lecture about European values, and your story of your family's errors down through the ages gave me the 'connection' that Steve had told us to look for. What you said about Grace and the F.F.V. was probably true, but it would have been true in spades about the Brent sisters. You said that those generations of family yet to come would 'magnify any substantive decision tenfold.' That was the leverage that would make killing the least distressing of a whole number of options. And the only people in our puzzle who had that kind of value system—that overwhelming motivation—were the two women."

Carson asked, "But why did they capitulate so easily? Why didn't they stonewall it, and say 'up your ear, peons, we don't care what anyone thinks'?"

"No, Edward was right about that risk," Lehman broke in, "because with tradition goes style. There are things that are done and things that are not done. And ways to do things and ways not to do things. The women had chosen a course. They watched it unfold and when they saw it was not going to work, they dropped it—with style. To bicker and lie and obfuscate would have degraded their role. It would have been distasteful. It would shrink them in their own eyes."

"Jesus Christ," said Carson.

"So what do you think actually happened with the killing, then?" Crighton asked.

"Yes, Edward," Lehman said, "what did happen?"

"Well, once you'd given us a set of values to work with, it became pretty easy to work backward. I suspect Steele called them before she came up here, made as distasteful a threat as possible to get them all stirred up, and then appeared on Wednesday morning. Rather than being panicked, as she hoped and expected, the two women had decided to see how much she knew and were probably prepared to eliminate her long before she even appeared. The nephew was off in New York, so they didn't have to worry about him.

"I suspect Steele arrived, was met in the Great Hall at the noon break between tours, and she staged her act. I can see the sisters exchanging one significant glance and peeling back the floor cloth. I suspect they opened the hidden door, and took her down to 'show her the long lost books' under the Hall. Steele gazes in awe at some rare gem, reaches up to lift it off the shelf—and is hit on the back of the head with the back of a hatchet—just like the hunting sisters would finish a fox. Probably Sarah, but Martha may be even more implacable.

"They stuff poor Steele in some trash bags, go out and dig inside their new compost fence, and await nightfall. At this point, they could claim the girl never arrived, and they know nothing about anything. Then the nephew comes home and the women assign him the task of moving the body and the car."

"Wouldn't he have gone screaming into the night yelling, 'I'm not going to get mixed up in this'?" Crighton asked.

"The books. Don't forget he's desperately eager to keep things quiet till he can get the books sold. No, I suspect the three of them struggled the body up and out the door—only to discover Grace's lights on and her wandering around at what is now past midnight. They must wonder what she has seen. What does she know? Should she be killed too? No, she's much too public. Her disappearance would bring everybody swarming in. Somebody must have thought, let's put the body under Grace's floor, and we can either use it to keep her quiet if she threatens to tell, or reveal it to the police to divert attention from the murderer. I suspect that scenario would have been Elliott's contribution to the situation."

Fairchild shuddered and put her hand over her mouth.

"Incidentally," George said, "I was going to do a great analysis over where all the keys were, yesterday. You did know that somebody—probably Elliott—had hidden them in your filing cabinet to direct suspicion toward you, didn't you, Grace?" George asked.

"No, I didn't know. Don't tell me things like that! Do you want to know what's even more ironic? I have a set of the keys to the Porsche on my key ring in my purse. I've never thrown them away from the days when we both drove the car together. They wouldn't have had to implicate me with Durr's set. I had my own and I could have moved the car without access to anything!"

"I think there's a lesson in that for all of us, but I'm too confused right now to figure out what it might be!" George laughed. "Tell me," he said, "in regard to your roommate's thesis: have you read it yourself?"

"No, but I've talked to people who have—advisors and some of the people on the board."

"How much of the existence of the books is revealed? Did she specify where the books are now?"

"Oh, no. She wanted to hold that close to exploit it for herself. All the thesis describes is the fact that at the time the Capitol was burned, the books were never injured, and that Jefferson's friends simply *claimed* they were lost so they could cover a transfer of Treasury funds to a particular individual. That was unconstitutional then, of course—and still is, for that matter. You have to transfer tax money through programs that are equally available to all people. They had to find some way to make it look like Jefferson was being paid for something, so they claimed the books went up in flames along with the buildings. No, Durr didn't even hint that the books still exist. She wanted to use that knowledge to get money for herself."

Crighton broke in. "What will you do now that she's no longer threatening everything? Will you stay on here?"

"I haven't really thought that far ahead, I've been so

involved in this mess. I guess I'll stick around and finish the transfer of Belvoir to the state, and then I might go back to Charlottesville and get the doctorate after all."

"Will you do the book thing yourself?"

"God, no! I hope never to breathe a word about that the rest of my life! No, I must admit I've gotten rather interested in the Fairfax family since I stumbled into here. I may concentrate on them for a while. I think there's a lot of material there that's never been explored."

Crighton laughed. "I guess I should tell you that when I was trying to find out about you and Durance Steele, I was told what a great impact you had had on the U.Va. social scene. My informant seemed to be looking forward to your return with great eagerness. You left a strong cheering section behind you. You'll be welcomed with open arms."

Grace Fairchild grinned and said, "You're too kind. Hey!" she said suddenly, "what time is it?"

"A quarter to two."

"I've got a tour to do in fifteen minutes! I suppose I can't turn off my life just because I've suddenly got it back. The visitors will be lining up on the walk."

George was struck by an inspiration. "Alexa, have you got the time and energy to see the house? It's magnificent, and considering all you know about its occupants, you really should see the mansion. Would you find this interesting?"

"That would be marvelous," she replied.

"Great!" Grace Fairchild said, "You all come on, and I'll give you my very best, solid gold lecture."

"You run on," George said, "we've got just one more matter of business to settle, and we'll meet you by the sign at two o'clock."

"Splendid. See you there, and, folks, thank you so very, very—"

"Get out of here," Carson and Crighton said almost together. "We'll catch up with you in a minute."

Chapter 28

"**F**AMILY," said Edward George, when the four were alone in the colonial kitchen, "we have our own ethical matter to decide. We have, through a strange series of unlikelies, become privy to an unknown piece of Americana. For a hundred and fifty years, the original Library of Congress has lain in that cellar there. The Brents aren't going to mention it. Grace Fairchild says she's not going to mention it, and I believe her—it nearly cost her her life. The police think we were just referring to some old books, and there are plenty enough of those spread around the public floors that they won't think any more about it. The mansion is about to be given to the state of Virginia, and my guess is that as long as that splendid sailcloth floor covering lasts, no one will ever look below the center hall. The official plans show it to be an unexcavated crawl space, and everyone thinks of it as a soil-filled crawl space. Not until the sailcloth comes off will anyone discover that door. Result? Those books could easily sit there another generation or two, completely unknown to history. Thus the question: do we 'tell'?"

Alexa said, "How would you 'tell'?"

George laughed with genuine amusement at the irony of it all. "Ha! You could hardly find four people more appropriate for telling this story! I have spent my life glorifying libraries, and 'the book' has been my most worshipped artifact. Here is a library that belonged to the American people, that represents a microcosm in amber of the thinking of the Founding Fathers, that 'belongs to the library profession.'"

"And Carson," said Crighton, "spends his whole life digging artifacts out of the ground and spreading them across museums till hell won't have it. God, what a coup! You'll never have to have another original thought the rest of your working life!"

"You should talk," he snapped back. "The number of press releases you can get out of this will take you right into your pension. The mind boggles with the way you can reveal this to a literate world—with your name in the upper left-hand corner of every one."

Alexa laughed with them. "And before any of you remind me of my links to the National Board for the Preservation of Antiquities, I will supply it myself."

"But," said George more solemnly, "I think we are all only too aware that we have just seen an amazing number of people almost crushed by the overtones of those books. There is no way of telling the story without taking a bit of the luster off of Thomas Jefferson's generous gift to the nation, or of the Library of Congress's glorious history, or of the care by which the Brent family loyally kept the secret hidden for so long."

"But," Carson said, "the existence of the books is truth. Is it morally defensible for four people to bury truth? Is it for us to say? Doesn't history require it to be put in a public place with the light on and let the *public* decide?"

"I would be more sensitive to the books as property,"

Crighton said. "They belong to the People . . . to the government . . . to Congress . . . to the Library of Congress . . . to . . . to *someone*. They didn't disappear. They're real. They were taken from somebody, and they've got to go back to somebody."

Dead silence.

Finally Lehman asked, "What good would they do anyone? Are there any books there that the world has never seen?"

"Almost certainly not," George said. "Just one more copy—presumably in better condition than what anyone else has."

"As far as preservation goes," Lehman said, "they're probably better preserved there than they would ever be again if they were brought out."

"That is the dilemma of all the marine archeology," Carson said. "As long as it's under seawater it lasts from generation to generation. As soon as it comes into the air, you get about two days of photographs and television clips and then it begins to crumble into dust. No matter how hard we try to case it in plastic and who-knows-what it's never as good again as when we brought it up. Once those books see light and feel city air they start to die."

"So we really aren't depriving our generation of anything, and in fact are preserving the materials for a thrilling experience for some future time," Alexa concluded.

"But it's not the books as books that matter," George said. "Will our understanding of Jefferson, or our national pride, our sense of the library's traditions be better served exposing what we know?"

Much longer silence.

Finally broken by Crighton Jones. "I say we forget the whole thing. The memory of it all stays here in this room surrounded by the smell of ashes and brick dust and aging wood from two hundred years ago. Somebody else can find them."

Carson nodded. "I'm with you."

"And I," said Alexa.

George frowned. "It bothers me that we have arrogated to ourselves the yea or nay on such an important matter, but as for the decision itself, I am in complete agreement. The missing Library of Congress book collection can be found by someone else another generation down the line."

Without a word, almost involuntarily, they extended their hands and held them in a single clasp, relishing the warmth of each other's fingers against their own.

Alexa said with a little smile, "And then there is a quote from Seneca that comes to mind. It is left over from a classical education that may or may not have been worth the agony I expended on it when I was too young to fight back. Apropos of both our decision and the decision made by those friends of Thomas Jefferson so long ago, Seneca said: 'Successful and fortunate crime is called virtue.'"

At two o'clock, they joined Grace Fairchild and a group of visitors on the oystershell walk beside the guide's office. Fairchild was smoothing the creases out of her uniform in the manner that had given Carson such pleasure, and she was saying, "As you can see, the house is one of the most beautiful Georgian buildings in the country. It was built in 1741, and still looks almost exactly the way it did when . . ." She gave her friends a warm, deliberate wink, and continued with the lecture.

How Much of This Is True?

Answer: All of it, except for one thing.

All the historical data—that is, all the information up to the twentieth century—is correct. The one thing that is not accurate is the use of Belvoir Mansion as the site of the lost books. Belvoir was gutted by fire in 1783, leaving only the walls standing, and these were shelled to the ground in 1814 by a British naval force in the Potomac, who mistook the silhouetted walls for some kind of fortification. The HABS measured drawing is real enough, but it consists solely of the cellar walls, which still exist (filled with soil to preserve them), flush with the ground. If readers would like to work on the same puzzle, they will have to find their own house. My 'Belvoir' isn't going to cut it.

The various documents in Chapter 6 are indeed accurate and exact, and appear in the official *State Papers of the United States*. They were rediscovered in 1981. The absence of contemporary reference to Jefferson's offer of the books and to the congressional purchase itself is equally real and as of this writing, inexplicable.

But do the books still exist? Did they survive the burning of the Capitol?

If anybody knows, they're not telling. Until they do, your and my guesses are as good as anyone else's. Good hunting!

C.G.